# BRANDED:
## (Revised Edition)
## An Old West Spanking Tale

C. C. Barrett

ISBN: 1453780203

Copyright 2010 & 2011© C. C. Barrett

All rights reserved.

No part of this book may be used or reproduced in any manner whatsoever without the expressed and written permission of the author.
This book contains adult situations and should only be purchased and read by those over 18 years of age.
All characters and events depicted in this book are fictional. Any similarities to any event or persons, living or deceased, is purely coincidental.

Dedication:

To my husband; I could not have done this without his support, acceptance and honest reactions.

# THE CATTLE DRIVE

## Chapter 1

    Amelia and her cousin, Bonnie, crept through the thick brush as they made their way down to the pond. The darkness was expected to break as sunrise was less than an hour away. The girls couldn't help themselves. The water looked too inviting as they passed it the night before.

They had been on the cattle drive for three days now, helping the cook as a means to get out West. Short on money, it was lucky they had met up with the cattle drive. They needed to work their way across the country if they had any hope of marrying men of their own choosing. The rancher, Ned Crowley, who led this particular drive, was a big burley man in his thirties. He was ruggedly handsome with a touch of gray at his temples. He disliked taking women on the drive. They were usually trouble and complicated the hell out of an already grueling trip. But with an injured cook he needed the help. He knew he couldn't keep his workers if he didn't have a warm meal for them every morning and every evening after a hard day of pushing cattle.

He took the girls on as his wards with the expressed agreement that he expected complete obedience and they wouldn't go wandering off or venturing far from the wagon without expressed permission. He was very clear that any disobedience would be met with a heavy hand. He, in turn, would insure their safe passage and make sure none of his cowboys got out of line.

The girls were a bit inexperienced, but Amos the cook, kept them busy with his instructions as he recuperated from his broken arm. The girls slept in the chuck wagon as Amos was ordered to sleep underneath to discourage any ranch hands from getting to familiar with the young women. The cook resented giving up his warm bed inside the wagon. The cold hard ground made his bones ache and his muscles sore. He took to drinking a little whisky, which explains why he didn't hear Bonnie and Amelia sneak out of the wagon before sunrise.

"We're almost there!" Amelia squealed in delight as the spring fed pond came into view.

"Oh, it will be so good to get clean," Bonnie said as she began untying her hair from its ponytail.

As they neared the edge of the water, they deposited their towels and began to undress.

The two peeled off every stitch of their clothes. They shrieked as they slowly made their way into the cold water. The tiny waves lapped at their bare bodies with each step. Amelia, the more adventurous one, was the first to plunge head first underwater. Bonnie yelped as she was drug under, when her cousin playfully pulled her feet out from under her.

"I wish we had time to clean our clothes," Bonnie said as Amelia nodded in agreement.

"This will have to do. We're taking a big enough chance just coming here. Mr. Crowley would be awfully mad if he knew we snuck off," Amelia warned.

"But why can't we stay a few days?" Bonnie whined.

"You heard Mr. Crowley. He has to get these cows to the market before the price drops. Besides it wouldn't be safe for us to travel alone," Amelia replied as she soaped her hair and body.

"I don't care about those smelly cows; I just want to be in clean clothes," Bonnie pouted.

"Don't think about that. Just think about the men we're bound to meet when we get out west. They say there are ten men for every one woman. We will have our pick!" Amelia exclaimed, just before she dunked her head under to rinse her hair.

"Hand me that soap if you're finished," Bonnie requested.

The girls splashed and giggled as they fantasized about how their lives would be when they finally got settled with husbands. They reminisced about their days in boarding school. When they each received telegrams from their parents, ordering them to return home after graduation to prepare for marriage to men neither of them had met, the girls decided that they would head west instead. Amelia found an advertisement for mail order brides on the bulletin board at the post office. Convincing Bonnie that the territory had to be desperate for women, Amelia hatched a plan for them to work their way out west without the ties of matrimony that came with being a mail order bride. The girls had hopes for adventure and to be able to marry a man of their own choosing when they were good and ready.

As they swam and dove into the cool waters, neither noticed the sun rising slowly over the tree tops.

✳✳✳

"Where's breakfast?" Crowley asked Amos.

"I'm doin the best I can Boss," the cook growled while he placed a Dutch oven full of biscuits on the fire.

"Where's your helpers?" Ned asked as he poured a cup of coffee.

"Haven't seen em this mornin," Amos grumbled, resenting the girls.

"Were they here when you got up?" Crowley asked as he took a seat on a nearby stump.

"Nope," Amos short answered.

"Any idea when they left?" the boss inquired, growing concerned.

"Nope, but they was here around five this mornin when I got up to shake the dew off my lily," the cook said as he put a large frying pan full of bacon on the fire.

"I put you in charge of keeping an eye on them. Do you have any idea where they might have gotten off to?" Crowley asked, trying to keep his temper in check.

"I told ya I ain't no babysitter. Have ya checked with the cowboys?" Amos asked, getting plain frustrated by being raked over the coals because of the girls.

"No, I gave them strict orders to leave the girls alone," Ned answered, standing up and finishing off his cup of coffee.

"Yeah, but ya didn't tell those girls to leave THEM alone," Amos pointed out.

"Have the men that come in for breakfast split up and ride out in each direction to search for the girls. Females are nothing but trouble. I swear, I wish I'd never brought them along," Crowley said angrily as he plopped his cowboy hat on his head and went to saddle his horse.

Amos grinned, taking great pleasure in knowing his "helpers" were in hot water with the boss. They'd wasted enough food during the meal preparations to feed twice their number and he knew he'd get an ass chewing when Crowley found out they needed to restock supplies ahead of schedule.

"What's for breakfast?" Toby Hanson asked as he and several other cowpokes came up to warm their hands by the fire.

"Nothin til the girls get back," Amos said as he shook a stick in the air. "Boss wants you all to ride out and try to find em," he instructed the group of cowboys.

"Damn! But I'm hungry," Toby grumbled as he walked towards his horse.

✳✳✳

"We better get ba…" Amelia stopped mid sentence, as she saw Ned Crowley standing on the bank of the pond.

Bonnie ducked under the water hoping the rancher couldn't see that she was naked. Not sure what to do, Amelia treaded water and inched her way further from the shore. Mr. Crowley didn't look pleased as he watched the girls' heads bob up and down.

"Get out of the water," Crowley said angrily, hiding his relief of finding the girls unharmed.

"You go on back, we'll be right behind you," Amelia hollered.

"Get out NOW!" Ned's temper was clearly showing.

"Um, well you see…we…can't…We don't have any clothes on," Amelia replied, embarrassed by their predicament.

"Ya got no need of clothes for what you two got coming," the rancher said as he walked toward a nearby birch tree and began pulling off small limbs.

"What do you think he means by that?" Bonnie whispered to Amelia.

"I don't know," Amelia replied as she tried to make out what he was doing.

"Come on, get out. If I have to tell you girls again it'll just go harder on ya," they heard him say.

Slowly Amelia started swimming toward the edge of the pond with Bonnie right behind her. They stopped swimming when their feet touched the bottom. The slippery moss made it hard to stay upright.

"Aren't you going to turn around?" Amelia asked, trying not to lose her footing.

"Nope," Crowley said as he sat down on a large rock facing the girls.

"But we are completely naked!" Bonnie exclaimed as her face reddened.

"That'll save time," he said as he began tying the bundle of birch switches together with a piece of twine.

"I'm not going to get out with you sitting there watching us!" Amelia yelled indignantly as an uneasy feeling came over her.

"Have it your way. You can come out now or when my men arrive. Some of them haven't seen a naked woman in a while and I spect some have never seen one get her ass whooped," Ned stated bluntly.

The girls gasped at his last words. Bonnie looked at her cousin, fear clearly showing in her eyes. Amelia tilted her head high putting on a brave front. As if to challenge him, Amelia glared directly at Crowley as she began making her way toward him. Ned met her steady stare until only her feet were still in the water. He slid his eyes down her bare body taking in her pert breasts and her mound of dark curly pubic hair. Seeing the direction of his gaze, Amelia quickly tried to hide her nakedness from his discerning stare by putting her arm across her chest and a hand down toward the "V" of her legs.

"You don't need clothes right now," he said as Amelia made a move to retrieve her garments.

"What's that supposed to mean?" Amelia asked haughtily.

"I don't give whippings with clothes on," Crowley said evenly as he picked up the birch he'd finished making.

Amelia shivered as she saw the wicked looking implement in his strong hands. As she began backing away from him, she noted his enormous biceps that were stretching his shirt sleeves.

"Bend over this rock," he said as he stood up from his seat and moved to the side.

"I will NOT!" Amelia protested, distress evident in her voice.

"You can do it now while it's just us or you can do it when the cowboys get here. It's up to you, but mark my words, you are both gonna get a whippin,'" he warned.

Amelia glanced around nervously to see if anyone was watching. She saw Bonnie staring at her from the water. She timidly approached Crowley. He positioned her over the big boulder so her bare bottom was sticking out. Amelia waited for the first blow to fall, anxiety clearly written on her face.

"Why are you being punished?" he asked, still holding the birch down by his side.

"Because we wanted to get clean," Amelia answered sarcastically.

She heard the wisp of the switches, as they went through the air, before they made contact with her bare behind. Amelia held a brave face as the burning in her ass cheeks began to build.

"Try again," Crowley commanded.

"Because we went for a swim," Amelia answered again, a bit less surly.

Three quick swishes of the birch came raining down on her ass leaving thin lines across each cheek. Amelia bit her lip to keep from crying out. Her stubborn streak refused to allow him the satisfaction of knowing he was causing her discomfort.

"Try again," he said, clearly running out of patience.

"Because we disobeyed you and left camp," Bonnie yelled from the water's edge, hoping to appease the rancher and possibly spare her cousin and herself from further punishment. Ned turned toward Bonnie and nodded his approval.

"That's right young lady but I want her to say it," he said as he pointed at Amelia.

Amelia stood and turned to face Crowley. She made no attempt to hide her nakedness or her rebellious attitude.

"You got your answer," Amelia said hotly.

"You will admit your wrongdoing or we'll be here all day," Ned said evenly as he motioned for her to get back into position.

She eased back over the rock. An involuntary gasp escaped her lips when she felt his foot ease her legs apart. Her face flooded with embarrassment as her womanhood was completed exposed to him.

"Let's start over," Ned said. "Why are you being punished?"

Amelia clenched her teeth, refusing to answer. She was startled by how hard Crowley brought the birch down on her this time. After four strokes Amelia began to feel her resolve give way. She could see Bonnie still standing in the water pleading with her eyes.

"We left camp!" Amelia sharply responded, angry with herself for giving in.

"Partly, but why else?" Crowley asked.

When she didn't answer him right away he laid three more harsh strikes to her striped backside.

"We disssooobeyyyed," she cried.

"Who did you disobey?" he asked as he struck her again.

"YOUUU!" Amelia yelled out as the stinging in her bottom intensified beyond belief.

Her fanny was a mixture of purple and red welts. Ned laid the birch to her three more times before ordering her to get up. Amelia stood and quickly brushed away the tears that were streaming down her face.

"Go stand facing that tree," he ordered, pointing to an oak tree about five yards away.

Amelia did as she was told without argument. She rubbed her fiery backside as she looked in Bonnie's direction. Her cousin hadn't moved from the water, but tears where running down her cheeks as she hugged herself, visibly quaking where she stood.

"Your turn," Ned said as he looked toward the frightened young woman.

"Please Mr. Crowley, we won't disobey you again," she pleaded from her firmly planted spot in the water.

"I hope you mean that, but it's time for your punishment, now come here," he ordered.

When she didn't make a move in his direction she expected him to come into the water and drag her out. He surprised her by just staring silently at her. She finally began to slowly, almost involuntarily, move towards her waiting fate. Shaking all over, she laid across the boulder as Amelia had done a few moments before.

"What will happen if you disobey me again?" Ned asked calmly.

"I will be punished," she immediately said as she felt the sting of the birch across her bare cheeks.

"Owwweee," Bonnie screamed as the tiny limbs cut into her flesh again.

"Who will punish you?" Ned asked, flailing her again.

"You," she quickly said as three more swats with the angry birch caught her square on her bottom.

Bonnie jumped up off the rock and began to dance around holding her backside.

"Get back over that rock," he said as he pointed for her to resume her position.

"Pleeease, no more, I'll be good," Bonnie pleaded as she backed away from the rancher.

"Let's get this over with," he said tenderly, as if dealing with a child.

Amelia turned her head to look at her cousin. Bonnie hung her head dejectedly as she stumbled toward Ned. He helped her bend over the rock again as she submitted to further punishment.

After several more lashes of the birch, Ned was finished chastising his wayward wards.

Bonnie's bare cheeks flamed with the same red and purple welts as those of her cousin. Just as the last stoke was laid to Bonnie's ass, horses could be heard approaching. Bonnie went to rise but the Ned Crowley quickly stopped her.

"Don't get up," he ordered. "And don't you turn around," he told Amelia as five of his cowhands swiftly approached on horseback.

"We heard screaming," Toby said as he stopped short in front of the trail boss.

Toby grinned, as understanding came over his face, when he spied the two girls with striped bottoms. Ned glanced around to make sure the women were facing away from his workers with only their asses on display. The men on horseback were fascinated by the sight of the two pair of round naked globes presented before them. The hard saddle reminded them of their discomfort as their natural response to the naked female form grew.

Bonnie continued to sob softly and her face took on a red glow of embarrassment, having been seen in such a position by the group of men. Amelia leaned her head against the oak, wishing she could melt into the tree trunk.

"Leave me a horse and round up the other men," Crowley ordered. "Tell them the girls have been found," he added as the men rode away, some glancing back for one last look.

"You girls get dressed," he ordered, watching them slowly turn to face him. "I hope I don't have to ever do that again," he continued, "but I will if need be."

Turning his back to them he walked a few yards away so they could get dressed. His own stiffened cock needed time to relax before getting into his saddle.

When they were dressed he announced it was time to get back to camp. Knowing a horseback ride would make a further impression of their punishment upon their roasted backsides, he made them ride double all the way to camp at a fast trot.

Bonnie and Amelia weren't accustomed to riding horses, especially totting through the unfamiliar terrain. Their moans of discomfort and pleas to walk went ignored as Ned was determined to make up the time they had cost him.

When they arrived back at camp, the cook had breakfast ready. Most of the men were already sitting around eating as Ned and the girls rode in. Grins and snickers were heard as the girls dismounted and their embarrassment quickly returned. Amos was in an unusually good humor.

"Get them dishes clean," he demanded as he smacked Bonnie on the rear when she passed by.

"None of that!" Crowley yelled at Amos. "I'm the only one that disciplines around here," he said as he looked at each and every one of his men. "Got that?" he asked sternly. "Any of you who touch one of these girls without my say so will answer to me and I will do more than just tan your hide."

When the girls heard this, they looked at each other and smiled.

# THE CRITTERS

## Chapter 2

It was almost dusk and Ned had decided to camp three hundred yards from the river they had crossed late that afternoon. They would head out the next morning when everyone was fresh. Even with the chill in the air the two young women, Amelia and Bonnie, requested to go take a bath in the river. A good birching to their bare bottoms taught them a lesson in their first week not to leave camp without permission. The exasperated rancher directed them to a bend in the river that would give them some privacy and told them to be quick about it. They still had to help Amos prepare supper.

The rancher had regretted his decision to allow the girls passage several times over. The girls can get into trouble faster than a rattlesnake can strike, he thought to himself. Ned, being a gruff man, wasn't very tolerant of their antics. He would not hesitate to reign with a stern hand if needed to keep the girls in line and his cattle drive moving. He made it clear right from the start of what he expected from the girls and that if they were to be a part of the drive they were expected to obey the rancher without question. Any disobedience or misbehavior would be met with strict discipline. Punishment was something Ned Crowley would not hesitate to dispense. Without a doubt Amelia and her cousin Bonnie had become a pain in his ass; he smiled at the irony.

***

The water was so cold the girls didn't take long to get last week's dust rinsed off. On their way back to camp they came across a hollowed out tree. Hearing unusual mewing noises, Bonnie peered in to find three tiny baby animals crying. They all had the same markings, black with a single white stripe down their back.

"Kittens," the girls squealed with delight as they picked them up and gently petted each one.

Bonnie, not having the heart to leave them alone, decided to wrap them carefully in her towel and carry them the hundred yards back to camp. Amelia helped her place them in the wagon where they would sleep that night. The "kittens'" cries increased as they pattered around in the wooden confines. Mr. Crowley heard the noise and went to investigate as the girls were helping Amos fix supper.

"What have we got here?" he asked as he peered into the wagon calling the girls over.

"We found these kittens abandoned," Bonnie said with a smile.

"Aren't they the cutest things you've ever seen?" Amelia chimed in.

"They ain't kittens!" the rancher exclaimed. Hearing him raise his voice, some of the cowpokes, out of curiosity, came over to the wagon.

"SKUNKS!" Toby shouted with a hoot. The other cowboys laughed as they slowly eased back from the wagon.

"Get them out of here, right now," Mr. Crowley ordered.

"What do we do with them?" Amelia asked, hurt that they were being laughed at.

"Take them back to where you found them!" Crowley commanded.

Bonnie climbed into the wagon and began handing the tiny creatures down to Amelia's waiting arms. When Amelia only had two she looked questioningly up at Bonnie. Her cousin put her finger to her lips.

"I'm keeping one," Bonnie whispered.

"You better not," Amelia warned sharply.

"Shhhhhhhh," Bonnie said as she climbed down out of the wagon. The girls headed back to the hollowed out tree and placed the two baby skunks inside. With a sad look on her face, Bonnie headed back to camp with Amelia.

"I'm coming back for them if they are still there in the morning," Bonnie whispered to her cousin. Amelia just shook her head in disbelief. Bonnie had a soft spot for all animals and there was no sense in trying to change her mind.

That night Bonnie curled up with the baby skunk, trying desperately to keep it quiet. She was afraid its pitiful cries would be heard.

"It's probably hungry," Amelia said as she rolled over trying to cover her ears.

"HUSH up there," Amos whispered harshly as he thumped the bottom of the wagon with his foot.

✷✷✷

"BLAST IT TO HELL!" Ned bellowed early the next morning as he got up from his bed roll. All the ranch hands sat up with a start. The commotion startled the momma skunk that had wondered into the camp that morning in search of her baby. She began spraying every which way as the cowhands scrambled out of their bed rolls and ran backwards holding their noses. Not a single man was spared from the odious spray except for Amos, who was still sleeping soundly under the wagon.

The girls woke to the sight of the momma skunk and her two babies standing in the middle of their camp. Amelia gave a heavy sigh in Bonnie's direction.

"I told you that keeping that baby skunk was not a good idea," Amelia said to her stunned cousin.

"What in tar nation is all that racket about?" Amos asked groggily as he crawled out from under the wagon.

He got out from under the wagon and saw Bonnie trying to hide her little "kitten." Bonnie looked at the cook guiltily and pleaded with her eyes for him not to give her away. With a grin he called the boss over to the wagon.

"I spect this is what old momma skunk is looking for," Amos declared to his boss as he tattled on Bonnie and pointed inside the wagon. Ned eased slowly around the momma skunk, grimacing at the odor that now engulfed the entire camp.

"Hand it over," he ordered as he looked sternly at Bonnie.

Bonnie gently picked up the baby skunk and placed it in the rancher's hands.

"Please don't hurt it!" she exclaimed as he cradled the tiny creature before easing it down on the ground. It quickly scampered over to its mother. To everyone's relief the mother skunk and her three babies waddled off into the woods.

"PEEUUUU!" Amos yelled as he wrinkled his nose.

"Everyone to the river," Ned ordered as his cowpokes headed down toward the water to try to rinse off the rancid smell. "You girls stay put. I'll deal with you when I get back," he said ominously over his shoulder as he left.

"I told you not to keep it!" Amelia grumbled at Bonnie. "Now we're in trouble."

"I'm sorry Amelia. I just couldn't help myself."

"I'm sure that excuse will go over real well with Mr. Crowley," Amelia said sarcastically, clearly aggravated with her cousin.

"What do you think he'll do to us?" Bonnie asked with fear creeping into her voice.

"Us?" Amelia asked. "I didn't do anything," she added, wondering if the rancher would see it that way.

Overhearing the girls' conversation, Amos snickered to himself knowing the girls were in for real trouble. No one disobeyed the boss and got away with it. He had heard the gossip of how Crowley had blistered their bare asses for leaving the camp last week. Toby, one of the youngest cowboys, told him that both girls were naked and their bottoms striped red when he and four others came upon the trail boss and the girls by the pond. Amos remembered how Toby's eyes glazed over as he recounted the sight of Bonnie's naked backside as she was bent over a boulder.

Bonnie caught Toby staring a time or two at her but she would quickly look away, embarrassed at knowing he had seen her punished flesh.

Amos noticed the way the two eyed each other. He suspected that Toby was sweet on the girl and wouldn't be surprised if the young cowpoke replayed the sight of Bonnie's well rounded fanny over and over each night. Amos thought highly of Toby and hoped he wasn't headed for trouble.

"Do you want us to come down and help with breakfast?" Amelia asked, pulling Amos' attention away from his thoughts.

"Boss said for you all to stay put. If I was you I'd do as I was told this time. You girls are in enough trouble as it is," he said sharply. Seeing the color drain from Bonnie's face, he smiled to himself knowing his words had their desired effect.

Amelia patted her cousin's arm after seeing her distress and sighed heavily. She had been trying to come up with a plausible excuse for the remaining baby skunk to be in the wagon. She wasn't sure if her creativity failed her or if she was just too freighted to lie to Ned Crowley. Since the incident at the pond, she had been especially attentive whenever the trail boss was around. She would catch herself staring at his large biceps and long, muscular legs. She once caught him with his shirt off early one morning splashing water on his face and chest. She was mesmerized by the sight of his bare torso, strong back and broad shoulders. Amelia was not ordinarily attracted to gruff burly men but he fascinated her all the same. At night she would sometimes visualize the time he spanked her with the birch switches. She could understand feeling the phantom stinging of her bottom at the very thought, but the wetness between her legs confused her. She wondered if Ned Crowley has the same effect on Bonnie but Amelia was too embarrassed to talk to her about it.

*** 

The wet and cold cowpokes returned one by one from the freezing river. Some eyed the girls curiously and others just simply glared and grumbled in their direction. Breakfast forgotten, they wasted no time in packing up camp, wanting to move on away from the lingering stench of the skunk scent. When Bonnie caught Toby looking sadly in her direction she began to shiver.

"Do you think the men know what Mr. Crowley plans to do to us?" she asked with trembling lips.

"I don't know but I think we're about to find out," Amelia answered apprehensively as she spotted the rancher striding into the camp.

Bonnie reached for her cousin's hand and held tightly as they watched Ned walking around giving brisk orders to his ranch hands.

The girls began to relax as they soon found themselves moving slowly with the cattle drive as Amos guided the team of horses along at a slow and steady pace. Neither complained nor dared to point out that they had not eaten breakfast.

"Maybe going without breakfast is our punishment," Bonnie said hopefully.

"Maybe," Amelia responded with a lot less certainty than Bonnie would have liked.

The day seemed to drag on. Morning slowly turned to afternoon with barely a notice as the band of cowboys, cattle and wagon didn't bother to stop for a mid-day meal. Amelia's stomach growled as she placed a hand over it, looking embarrassed. Bonnie smiled shyly as her stomach responded as if answering back. Eventually the girls dozed off as the wagon jostled along until Amelia was awakened by her cousin.

"You were moaning in your sleep, are you all right?" Bonnie asked.

Amelia shook her head in reply. As if her erotic dream materialized before her eyes, Amelia watched breathlessly as Ned Crowley approached on horseback. Without glancing at either girl, he rode up to Amos and said something that only the cook could hear. They knew it was about them when Amos turned and gave them a sly smile as if he now knew a secret. Bonnie reached for her cousin's hand as her anxiety returned.

❋❋❋

By the time the cattle drive stopped for the night, Amelia and Bonnie were bone tired and every muscle ached from pent up anxiety and sitting in the wagon all day. Amos ordered them to help with supper. It was a quiet meal as everyone was on edge as if waiting for the loud clap of thunder after a lightning strike. The girls dished out beans and venison with shaky hands as the tension mounted. Amos frowned as food spilled on the ground. When the girls were cleaning up after the meal, they jumped when Amos came over and told them Mr. Crowley wanted to see them. With dread, the girls hesitantly walked over to where the rancher was waiting on the other side of the wagon. Toby watched as Bonnie dejectedly made her way towards the trail boss. He wanted to reassure her or comfort her in some way but knew she deserved to be punished. The other cowboys had been gossiping and speculating about their punishment all day. Some thought it was only right for Crowley to whip them in front of the entire camp, since it was their fault everyone and everything smelled of skunk.

      Ned had no reservations about upturning their bottoms for a good spanking. The whipping was the only thing he was sure about. The location was the real question. He made the girls wait all day hoping the anticipation of the punishment would further impress upon them to be obedient. He also wanted to buy himself time to cool his temper and decide the best way to approach the situation. He reminded himself several times that day never again to take women along on the trail. He heard the grumbling of his men and knew most were in favor of him disciplining the girls in front of the entire camp. He opted for a compromise as he stood on the farthest side of the wagon out of eye sight, but not out of earshot. The men could not see, but they could definitely hear what was going on, and that would have to be enough to satisfy them.

He watched as the girls approached him slowly. They both stopped suddenly and their eyes widened when they saw he already held his thick wide belt in his hand.

"Here," he said as he pointed for them to stand in front of him.

The girls each took a deep breath and faced him. Amelia met him head on, her eyes never wavering from his. Bonnie, on the other hand, was shaking considerably as her head hung down and she wrung her hands.

"I'm sorry," Bonnie suddenly wailed as tears began to stream down her face. "I know it was wrong to keep the baby critter but…please I won't do it again," she continued to beg, hoping he would relent and take pity on her.

"So it was you who disobeyed me?" he asked Bonnie.

Bonnie could only shake her head up and down.

"What about you?" he asked, staring into Amelia's eyes.

"It was just me, only me," Bonnie piped in before her cousin could answer.

Shocking Bonnie and Ned, Amelia shook her head in disagreement.

"No, I could have returned the skunk but I didn't. I knew all along that we kept it," she admitted with a brave tilt of her head.

Ned had to look away so she could not see his admiration of her confession. He almost relented on Amelia's punishment but suddenly a whiff of the skunk's remnant odor on his shirt caught his attention. With renewed resolve he motioned for Amelia to turn around.

"You're first," he said to Amelia. "Bonnie you're gonna watch and know I plan on going twice as hard on you."

Bonnie visibly shuddered as she stood aside, while he positioned her cousin and ordered Amelia to bend over and place her hands on her knees. Without any hesitation, he brought his belt down across her clothed bottom. Amelia winced slightly but kept her hands on her knees and her bottom protruding out. He laid his leather hard across her bottom five times before he stopped. Thinking her punishment was over; Amelia rose and began rubbing her tingly bottom.

"Pull up your dress," he ordered harshly, his tone catching Amelia by surprise.

Without protest, Amelia reached for the hem of her dress and bunched it up to her waist. Not waiting his instructions, she repositioned her hands on her knees and waited. Ned smoothed the material of her bloomers over her pink bottom. Amelia gasped as she heard the whoosh of his belt as it passed through the air before making contact with her backside. Without the added protection of her skirt she could feel the sting of the leather burn through the thin material. After five more slaps of the belt Ned stopped again. Amelia brought her hands behind her to rub her glowing backside. The tears in her eyes threatened to escape.

"Now take your bloomers down," Ned commanded loudly.

The cowboys' snickering could be heard yards away. Her face reddened as she slowly tugged her bloomers down to her knees. Bonnie turned away, unable to watch any longer.

Amelia was sure the crack of the leather could be heard all through the camp as Ned brought his belt across her bare ass three more times. Amelia tried to stay in place but after the last particular hard strike she couldn't help but dance around and cry.

"Back in position," she heard Ned say as she bent back over wondering how much more her butt could withstand.

After two more very hard blows, and being pleased with the glow of Amelia's round globes, Ned declared her punishment complete. Amelia slowly pulled up her bloomers and winced as the material scraped her flaming backside. She let her skirt fall and stood to the side as Ned motioned for Bonnie to come forward.

Bonnie thought she was going to be sick even though she had barely eaten a bite of supper. Her anxiety was overwhelming her and she began to hyperventilate. Amelia watched helplessly as her cousin stood before the rancher and shook from head to toe, gasping for air.

Ned Crowley wanted to take pity on the girl but his resolve wouldn't let him. After all, he rationalized, he whipped Amelia and she wasn't the true culprit. Knowing that most of the guilt lay with the shaking woman who stood before him, he ordered Bonnie to bare her bottom completely. Bonnie began to sob softly as she pulled her skirt, along with her bloomers, down to her ankles. The snickers from the cowpokes grew louder, which only added to her distress.

"Please Mr. Crowley, I'm sooo sorrry," she cried. "I…" but her words failed her as she bent forward and presented her bare backside.

Amelia watched and nervously bit her fingernails as Ned swung his belt back and brought it down against Bonnie's butt cheeks with a loud THWACK. At the first swat, Bonnie jumped up and screamed holding both cheeks with her hands, not caring that her skirt and bloomers were off completely and lying on the ground. Laughter could be heard coming from the other side of the wagon.

"Get back in position," Ned ordered as he pointed to the spot in front of him. Bonnie shook her head and backed away slowly.

"Please," Amelia implored her cousin. "Do as he says or it will go twice as bad for you."

"I CAN'T," Bonnie protested wildly.

"You WILL or I'll get some help from those cowboys over there," Ned said sternly as he pointed beyond the wagon.

Bonnie took a deep breath, trying to calm herself. Ignoring the hooting from the nearby men, she resumed her position and placed her shaking hands on her knees. Using all her might she remained in position for the next ten smacks of Ned's belt, tears streaming down her face.

Her bottom was lined with welts as each bite of the leather struck her unprotected rump. After the eleventh lick, she slumped to the ground and sobbed hysterically.

Losing patients, he made a motion towards the cowboys who were now listening with anticipation. Each hoped that they would be called upon to help administer the much deserved spanking. Ned stopped when Amelia reached out and grabbed his arm.

"Please let me help her," she begged with tears in her eyes.

"Help her up," Ned said after thinking it over quickly.

The groans of disappointed cowpokes could be heard clearly on the far side of the wagon.

Amelia helped Bonnie to her feet, all the while whispering encouragement in her ear. She held Bonnie's hands as the girl leaned over preparing for the remainder of her punishment. Ned made the last four whacks quick. He struck just below the underside of her bottom each time, ignoring Bonnie's howls.

When the rancher began to loop his belt through his pants, Amelia helped her sobbing cousin get dressed. Seeing the angry red welts, Amelia knew it would be several days before Bonnie could sit comfortably.

"The next time your disobedience affects this whole camp, I just might let the cowboys have a turn whipping your asses," he said quietly to both girls before he turned and walked away.

The girls shook their heads in acknowledgment, thankful that the ranch hands could not hear his threat.

Seeing the gawking cowpokes as they appeared from behind the wagon, the girls quickly realized if the men had heard Ned's remark each cowboy would be looking for any excuse to tattle on them. The knowing grin on some of the cowboys was the ultimate humiliation. Bonnie pushed passed Amelia as she rushed though the camp, sobbing into her hands. Ned put a hand on Amelia to stop her from going after her cousin.

"Let her be," he said gently as he watched Bonnie take up sulking against a tree on the far side of the camp. The cowboys whispered and glanced in her direction, only making matters worse. Bonnie could see Toby staring silently into the fire, not meeting her eyes.

"Why were you so hard on her?" Amelia asked as she recounted Bonnie receiving fifteen whacks on her bare bottom while she only got five on the bare.

"Bonnie was more at fault," he stated simply, not in the mood to discuss it, as he walked away to get a cup of coffee.

"Turned them bottoms red I spect," Amos said as he filled the rancher's cup, wishing he could see for himself the damage done to the girls backsides. "Could hear their squalling a mile away as you laid into them," Amos went on with a gleam in his eye.

"'Specially that girl there," Ned responded as he pointed in Bonnie's direction and grimaced wishing he'd never agreed to allow the women along. "Keep them busy and don't go easy on them just cause they got sore backsides," Ned said to the cook as he walked away to stand by the fire.

"Ya can count on me boss," Amos replied with a grin.

"May I go to my cousin now?" Amelia asked meekly as she approached Ned a little while later.

"Nope, she needs to tough it out," Ned said flatly.

"Are you sure she'll be alright?" Amelia asked, concern inching its way into her voice.

"She'll be fine," Ned replied confidently. "I suspect her pride hurts more than her backside right now."

"Well mine ain't feeling too fine right now I can tell you that," Amelia said flippantly as she absently rubbed her still stinging bottom.

Ned grinned at her remark, thinking of her plump red cheeks, wishing he could do more than just spank them.

Coming to a decision, Toby surprised everyone when he abruptly got to his feet and stalked with determination to the water barrel. Wetting his handkerchief with the cool water, he purposefully walked over to Bonnie and handed it to her. No one could hear what was said but every eye was on her as she took the wet cloth and disappeared behind the bushes. Toby stood guard with his back to the bushes as the girl slipped her bloomers down and put the cold cloth to her burning ass cheeks. Toby gave a hard stare at the others, daring any of them to come near for a closer look.

Ned groaned outwardly as he witnessed this act of chivalry. His head began to throb when he saw Bonnie emerge from the bushes and Toby's arm go around her protectively. A frown appeared on his face as the pair made their way towards the fire together. No one dared to comment when Bonnie gasped and winced when her bottom touched the hard ground as she tried to sit.

# THE COFFEE

## Chapter 3

After three weeks on the trail, the supplies were running low. On this particular day the winds were up and a steady chill had begun to sweep down the area. Amos and the girls were in a nearby town picking up supplies for the next leg of their journey as the cattle drive continued west. He gave special instructions to the women on how to load the wagon. Leaving them to it, Amos went down the street to the saloon to pick up one last necessary item to help rid the chill from his old bones.

"God these sacks are heavy," Bonnie said as she hoisted a fifty pound bag of flour up to Amelia.

Her cousin was stacking the dry goods at one end of the wagon, not following the cook's instructions.

"I don't think that's how Amos wants that stacked," Bonnie pointed out as Amelia dropped the bag of flour onto six other bags of dry goods that were piled so high they threatened to topple over.

"Then he should be here instead of over at that saloon," Amelia said snidely, still mad because Amos wouldn't allow them to look around the town and shop before heading back on the trail.

Amelia almost decided to go anyway except she knew the grouchy old bastard would waste no time in telling Ned. She wasn't prepared to pay the price of the hell fire Ned would rain down on her backside for a peek at the town and a few baubles.

The girls had been a pain in Amos' side ever since Mr. Crowley hired them on. They had no experience and he had no patience for giggly girls. They had to make this extra stop for supplies only because the women had wasted so much in the food preparations these last weeks. He didn't take kindly to being chewed out by the boss because the food ran out sooner than anticipated. The girls simply made his life miserable. To top it off they made him look bad to his boss. If it were up to him he would let them explore the town and leave them there to stay.

"Good riddance," he mumbled to himself before ordering a case of whisky from the bartender.

He was still grumbling when he hollered at Bonnie to come get the box of whisky and carry it to the wagon. With some difficulty he climbed up onto the wagon and just as they were ready to head out the merchant came running out.

"You're forgetting one," he exclaimed as he pointed to the seventy-five pound bag of coffee beans still sitting on the loading dock.

"Thanks. Can't leave that," Amos smiled kindly at the merchant. "Get your ass down there and get that sack," he barked at Amelia.

Amelia got down off the wagon with a groan and heaved the sack up only to lose her grip and the bag fell with a thud back to the ground.

"Hurry it up!" Amos shouted impatiently.

"I'm doing the best I can," she exclaimed as the bag fell to the ground a second time.

"Go help her!" he said as he gave Bonnie a hard nudged.

The two women each took hold of opposite ends of the bag and wrestled with it, trying to get it into the wagon. Unnoticed by either girl, a corner of the bag caught on a nail causing a tear about an inch long. They pushed and shoved it up until it finally landed with a plop on top of the other bags. The coffee beans poured slowly out onto the ground as the wagon headed out. Amos was in a hurry to catch up to the cattle drive, not wanting to make Mr. Crowley any angrier about this unexpected stop.

A few hours later the chuck wagon caught up to the cattle. They made good time and everyone seemed to be in good spirits by the time they stopped for the night. The night air had become exceptionally nippy and everyone helped collect firewood for the fire.

"Go get some coffee beans," Amos said almost pleasantly to Bonnie as he dug out the percolator. "It is gonna be a cold one tonight," he predicted as he filled it with water.

When Bonnie returned empty handed Amos looked at her questioningly.

"I thought I told you to get some coffee girl," Amos snapped.

"You did but I couldn't find any," Bonnie tried to explain.

"Nonsense! We just bought some," he growled as he stepped around to the chuck wagon to find the coffee.

"Need some coffee here," Ned hollered from the fire.

"Damn girls," Amos grumbled to himself as he climbed up into the wagon and began searching for the bag of beans.

"Where's the coffee?" the cowpokes asked as they settled around the blazing fire to keep warm.

"TARNATION!" Amos could be heard yelling from the wagon. "Look at what you girls done!" he barked as the supplies tumbled down around him. Some of the bags spilled open and flour and meal covered the bottom of the wagon bed. Bonnie glared at her cousin while Amelia looked down at the ground guiltily. They both couldn't help but reel with laughter when Amos slipped on the corn meal and fell on his backside.

With a roll of his eyes, Ned, followed by a few curious cowboys, went to see what the commotion was about.

"What is it?" Ned asked.

Then he saw his old cook knee deep in bags of flour, sugar and salt. Corn meal dusted his pant legs.

"It's them girls!" Amos shouted as he shook a fist at the women who were laughing so hard they had tears rolling down their faces.

"It's ruined! Most of the stuff is ruined and I can't find the darn coffee," he bellowed as he tried again to stand on the slippery meal.

"It can't be that bad," Ned said trying to calm Amos down.

"It IS, see for yourself," Amos replied.

The rancher peered over the edge of the wagon and stared at the supplies lying in disarray. Some of the bags were half empty as their contents spilled onto the wagon floor. With a heavy sigh he turned to look at the girls who didn't have enough sense to stop laughing.

"Help Amos out of that wagon and look for the coffee," Crowley barked at the nearest cowboy.

Recognizing that tone of voice, the girls ceased laughing immediately and stood by as the search for the coffee continued.

"Ahhh shhhit!" they heard Amos swear as he held up the empty coffee sack. "I knew we just bought a bag this morning," he said, eyeing the girls suspiciously.

"If you had stacked the supplies like I told ya…" he trailed off, shaking his head at the mess and examining the bag until he found the rip in the material. "We've been leaving a trail of coffee beans all day," he muttered as he angrily threw the sack down.

"What have you got to say for yourselves," Ned asked as he glared at Amelia and Bonnie, who didn't find the situation funny anymore, as all attention was brought to bear on them.

"We did the best we could," Amelia made the first attempt to explain.

"It was heavy and it must have ripped when we were loading it," Bonnie added with a whine.

"Most of these supplies are ruined," Ned said through gritted teeth. "We don't have any coffee because of your carelessness."

The girls could tell the rancher was becoming angrier by the minute. The grumbling from the other cowboys rose with the realization that they weren't getting any coffee tonight or the next morning.

"We'll have to make another supply run," Amos said, pointing out the obvious.

"We're a full two days away from any town," Ned said calmly, a bit too calmly. Amelia and Bonnie became nervous as he turned in their direction.

"What should I do about this?" he questioned the quiet girls.

Not sure how to appease the trail boss they mutely stared at the ground.

"I've got to pay for more supplies," he said, not believing his bad luck.

Ned stalked off, too angry to speak. The girls watched as he disappeared into the darkness. An uneasy calm settled over the camp as the remaining supplies were salvaged. The grumbling continued on as the evening grew colder. They all sat in silence wishing they had a hot steamy cup of coffee to warm them. Everyone was huddled around the fire and within easy listening when Ned reappeared in the firelight.

"I'm gonna take it out of your hides," he said firmly as he stood with his hands on his hips a few feet behind the girls. No one had to ask whose hides he was referring to.

"Get up and come with me," Ned said calmly.

The girls began to protest at once but he raised his hand to silence them. Not in the mood for excuses or explanations, he reached down and grabbed each girl by the arm and hauled them up on their feet. The cowboys stared as he led them to Amos who had been busy restacking the meager supplies with his one good arm.

"Amos, get your wooden spoon," Ned called to the old cook.

A confused look crossed the girls' faces as they watched Amos amble down from the wagon and fish out his long wooden spoon from the side box of the wagon. "Wooden spoon" wasn't giving it justice. The handle was close to two feet long and the end was more flat then spoon shaped. It was used for stirring food in the large iron kettles over the fire.

"Did you instruct these girls how to load the wagon?" Ned asked the cook.

"I surely did," he replied shaking his head.

"Did they do as they were told?" Ned questioned.

"Nope, they were too busy pestering me about exploring the town," Amos replied with disgust.

"What about this coffee?" Crowley asked.

"They were the last ones to take hold of it. I had no idea there was a hole in it or I would have done something," he answered, almost defensively.

"I'm not blaming you Amos," Ned quickly explained. "I just want to be sure I understand the situation fully before these girls are punished."

"They did it. Its cause of them we will be without coffee for a few days," Amos said, pointing to Bonnie and Amelia.

The girls mutely stood by as Amos recounted how sloppily they had stacked the supplies and how they had almost left the coffee entirely if it hadn't been for the merchant.

"Tonight you get to watch as I give these girls a good tanning with that wooden spoon," Crowley said.

Amelia and Bonnie began to talk at once, each trying to minimize their involvement in the supply catastrophe.

"Enough!" Ned said sternly, silencing the girls immediately.

"Which one of you goes first?" he asked, having made up his mind.

Since neither girl offered to be the first to be punished Amos pointed to Bonnie. Ned brought his left knee up and rested his foot on a stump. He motioned to Bonnie.

"Bonnie you first, bend over my knee," Crowley said.

Bonnie gave her cousin a furious look before she stepped timidly forward and laid her torso over Mr. Crowley's bended knee. Her feet barely touched the ground as he positioned her. Her clothed bottom perched high, ready to be punished. The first smack with the wooden spoon came as a shock as it vibrated through her backside. She wailed loudly as he continued to barrage her bottom with the wooden utensil. Amos watched with fascination as the girl began to wiggle with each hard whack from the trail boss. When Amelia's turn came, she stuck her tongue out at Amos before taking her place over Ned's leg.

"You get ten extra for that," Ned said as he began to strike her behind, the wood making hard cracking noises as it made contact with her skirted bottom.

Amelia resolved herself not to cry. She wouldn't give Amos the satisfaction. When Ned was finished he made the girls stand by the wagon for thirty minutes with their hands down by their sides. He gave them each a warning that he or Amos had better not catch them rubbing their bottoms. When the thirty minutes were up Ned came back to have a little talk with his arrant wards.

"That tanning was for tonight's coffee and the ruined supplies," he said. "You both get ten whacks each morning and each evening until we get close enough to a town to get supplies."

The girls gaped at his words, not believing they were in for several more punishment sessions before it was over.

Amos grinned when he heard what the boss had planned. If not for his need of caffeine he wished the next town was farther away.

\*\*\*

The next morning, after breakfast, the cowboys rode out to get the cattle moving. The girls breathed a sigh of relief when it was apparent that Ned had forgotten to administer his promised punishment for that morning. It wasn't until Amos hailed the boss over and reminded him that they were stopped from cleaning the dishes and ordered to bend over his knee once again. Ned gave each girl her ten quick licks with the freshly washed wooden spoon. They couldn't tell if Mr. Crowley was swatting harder or if the dampness of the spoon made each strike more painful that morning. They were just glad it was over and hoped they would come to a town very soon.

\*\*\*

By that evening the cowboys were noticeably more irritable. Even Mr. Crowley seemed particularly peeved at everyone and everything. The rancher didn't need a reminder that evening. When it was time for the girls' spanking they were surprised when he made them lift their skirts so he could whack their bottoms with just their bloomers for protection. The ten swats were even more torturous without the extra padding from their skirts and Mr. Crowley seemed to lay into them even harder than he did that morning. The girls cried softly when the rancher was through. Amos didn't know why the girls were making such a fuss. He thought the boss had gone easy on them and wished Crowley would allow him to tan their hides. He had spent a lot of time thinking on it as the trail grew long. He would bare their bottoms and after warming their asses until they were good and pink with the wooden spoon he would cut several switches and give them each such a tanning they wouldn't be able to sit until they got to the end of the trail.

Amelia and Bonnie were awoken by Amos earlier than usual the next morning.

"Get up the boss wants to see ya," he said crossly as he pointed to the far edge of the camp.

The trail boss woke Amos that morning and announced that the drive had to move out early because bad storm clouds were rolling in. The cowboys were tired and the lack of coffee was making everyone quick-tempered. A fight nearly broke out between two cowpokes and Ned was fit to be tied. The girls saw him standing on the edge of the clearing where they had made camp the night before. They could see he held the dreaded wooden spoon in one hand. Amos was instructed to get breakfast started, disappointed at not being allowed to watch as the girls were disciplined that morning.

"You deserve every lick," one outspoken cowpoke said as the girls walked by.

"…blister your behind," another spoke up.

Bonnie saw the young ranch hand, Toby, sitting by the fire as they passed by. He averted his eyes and bowed his head as they walked toward their fate. Her face reddened at the thought of him knowing she was being punished. She didn't care what the other's thought but she liked Toby and she valued his opinion of her.

When they reached Ned, he motioned for them to follow him down a path that was only visible to him. Ned led them to another clearing, far enough away from camp that no one could see them. The farther away from camp they went the more their anxiety grew. Their mouths fell open when he ordered them to remove their skirts and bloomers.

"This time I want your asses bare," he said angrily.

When the girls began to protest he threw the wooden spoon to the ground and both his hands went to his belt buckle.

"Wait, wait!" Bonnie was the first to recognize the precarious position they were in.

"Please not the belt," she pleaded.

Amelia looked petrified as she watched Bonnie peel off her skirt and bloomers. Mr. Crowley seemed especially cross this morning. Not having any caffeine for a few days did something to a man out on the trail, as the girls were about to find out.

"Bend over that log," Ned said as he pointed to a huge fallen tree that appeared to have been struck by lightning some years ago.

Bonnie quickly moved to obey him, not wanting to make the rancher any angrier. She presented her backside as he took no time in picking up the wooden spoon and striking it across both bare cheeks. She winced at the first swat and by the time he was on number ten she was shifting from one foot to the other sobbing wildly. Her contrition was barely audible through her wails. When her punishment was complete she was made to put on her skirt and bloomers over her throbbing rear and ordered to return to camp.

Amelia watched fretfully as her cousin quickly retreated out of sight. Amelia breathed deeply, looking for courage she didn't feel, and turned toward Ned. He was staring at her as if trying to work out a puzzle.

"Amos said you were the one stacking the supplies," he said quietly.

"I was," Amelia replied in a whisper, her lips trembling.

"Yet you let Bonnie take some of the blame," Ned stated.

"I never thought about it that way. We both handled the coffee sack," said Amelia.

"You deserve a harsher punishment than Bonnie," he said through gritted teeth.

Amelia breathed a long sigh and without a word began slowly taking her skirt and bloomers off. She painstakingly folded them and placed them neatly on the ground, ignoring her state of undress. Her delay tactics didn't go unnoticed by Ned. Neither did her rounded bare globes or her bushy triangle at the juncture of her legs. He was quickly running out of patience with this woman who was beginning to stir him to distraction.

"Over the log, NOW!" he growled more angrily than he actually felt.

Amelia placed her torso over the fallen tree and waited.

"Further over," he ordered as he positioned her bare bottom high in the air with her feet dangling.

The first swat came without notice and jarred Amelia, taking her breath away. Before she could recover, another hard swat with the spoon was laid across her cheeks. She wiggled her bottom left and right in an attempt to dodge the stinging of the wood.

"Stay still!" he commanded as he whacked her several more times in quick succession.

He let the wooden implement fall to the ground as he repositioned Amelia, bending her further over the log.

Amelia tried to calculate the number of strokes she'd received but lost count when he ordered her to spread her legs apart. Her face reddened as she was sure he could see her private parts. But her embarrassment was quickly replaced by scorching pain as he began smacking the underside of her cheeks with the palm of his hand. Ned didn't stop until her behind was flaming red and she was hollering loud enough to wake the dead.

When her punishment was over Ned allowed her to rest across the log for a few minutes. Absently he began to rub her back as she tried desperately to regain her composure. When her breathing resumed to an even tempo he helped her off the log. She immediately threw herself into his arms and the tears started again as she sobbed softly into his shoulder. Not sure what to do, he could only think to rub her back and assure her that everything was going to be alright.

"The punishment is over," he said softly against her ear. "Amos is on his way into town right now to pick up supplies," he said, continuing to hold her in his arms.

"You'll be a bit uncomfortable riding horseback today but the worst is over," he said as she continued to sniffle against his chest.

When Amelia looked up into his face he couldn't stop himself from brushing away the last of her tears with his calloused hand. He could see the trust in her eyes and without thinking he brought her face up to his and their lips touched for a brief moment. The spell was broken when they heard a rustling in the leaves. They quickly stepped apart and began to laugh when they saw two squirrels fighting over an acorn.

"You better get dressed," Ned said as he looked toward the sky, entirely too aware that Amelia was naked from the waist down. Amelia blushed at the mention of her state of undress and quickly put on her clothes. Ned focused all his attention on the squirrels as he tried to lessen his passion. He forced himself to divert his attention while the young woman he was alone with in the woods began covering her glorious backside. He peeked one last time at her bare ass and noticed Amelia wince slightly as she pulled her bloomers over her throbbing bottom.

When Ned was satisfied Amelia was decently dressed again, and his erection had diminished, he led her back to camp. Amelia felt admiration and respect as she followed him out of the woods. She felt all warm inside at his previous display of tenderness and looked forward to seeing more of this side of him.

However, she became confused by his sudden change in demeanor as soon as they arrived back in camp. Her romantic fantasies toward the rancher quickly turned sour as he briskly ordered her to mount a horse.

"We've wasted enough time and we need to move them cattle outta here before that storm gets here," he explained curtly as he rode off toward the moving herd.

"Ohhh….Ouch," Bonnie groaned as her sore bottom jostled in the saddle. "What took you so long?" she asked when Amelia was finally seated in the saddle.

Angered by Ned's sudden sharpness towards her, she didn't hesitate to put the rancher in an unflattering light by telling Bonnie how he had punished her ruthlessly; using both the spoon and his hand on her bare backside.

"Why?" Bonnie asked, confused by Amelia's pinched expression.

"Because he's a bastard!" Amelia shouted, looking in Ned's direction hoping he would overhear.

"SHHHHHHHH!" Bonnie exclaimed, shocked by Amelia's sudden outburst. "He'll hear you," she added, looking fearfully around, as if Amelia was about to be struck down by lightning.

"I hope he does," her cousin responded flippantly.

"He'll give you more than a taste of that spoon and the palm of his hand if you make him mad," Bonnie warned.

"I don't care!" Amelia shouted as she urged her horse into a gallop.

She rode about one hundred yards away when she couldn't stand the pain to her bottom any longer and eased the horse back to a slow and steady walk. Ned watched her galloping foolishness and made a mental note to discuss with her the recklessness of her actions.

He could picture her bent over his knee later that evening. His hands on her wiggling bare fanny, caressing at first and then soundly smacking each round upturned cheek hard enough to leave his hand print.

# THANK THE LUCKY STARS

## Chapter 4

"OUCH…Stop you're hurting me," Bonnie squealed.

"Stay still," Toby commanded.

"But it really, really hurts!" she yelled.

"Stop acting like a child," Toby said as he pulled another bur from her hair.

The two had slipped away from camp when the cattle drive stopped early that afternoon. The rain could be seen moving in across the plain. The trail boss didn't want to take any chances with the safety of his workers or the cattle with the threat of a flash flood. Toby had been looking for an opportunity to get Bonnie alone. The unexpected stop gave him just the chance he needed. They walked awhile until they came to a field. A game of chase ended with Toby catching Bonnie around the waist and pulling her to the ground. She was breathless and beautiful as Toby laid on top of her. His hand brushed the hair out of her face. The kiss caught Bonnie completely by surprise. She felt a funny feeling begin deep down and began to moan as his lips traced a trail down her neck. She froze when his hand went to her right breast. Slowly his hand reached for the hem of her skirt. He was stunned when he was pushed backward off her and landed on his butt. He looked confused until he caught the slightest smile shyly displayed on Bonnie's face. He grinned and lay down contently next to her, only their hands touching. Neither one spoke but just laid there feeling the tension build between them. Hearing the distant thunder, they sat up in unison to look toward the sky. The dark clouds were still far away. Toby looked at Bonnie and saw how disheveled she looked after lying in the field. He began pulling dried weeds and cockleburs from her hair.

"I am NOT a child," Bonnie said as she began to pout.

"You're acting like one, a spoiled brat even," Toby said as he pulled a weed from her hair.

"I can't help it, Mr. Crowley hates me," Bonnie pulled away and put her head in her hands.

"He doesn't hate you," Toby consoled.

"Then why does he beat me?" Bonnie asked lifting her head questioningly at the cowboy.

"He doesn't BEAT you, he gives you a good whipping for disobeying him," Toby said trying to sound older and wiser.

"Humph! What do you know?" Bonnie asked, beginning to pout again. "You should see my backside; it's black and blue…and…he hits me on my…um…"

"What?" Toby asked as his curiosity peaked.

"Um…he hits me on my…bare bottom," Bonnie finished in a whisper.

She knew Toby had seen her naked hindquarters after a good birching from the trail boss the first week she and her cousin joined the cattle drive. She felt excited and naughty bringing it up to Toby.

"Let me see it," Toby asked boldly.

"NO!" Bonnie shouted, pretending to be shocked by his request.

"Come on, I won't tell anyone," Toby begged as he tried to convince Bonnie to show him her bare ass.

Bonnie looked down at her lap for several moments thinking it over. Finally, after looking to see if anyone was about, she swiveled around facing away from the cowboy. He stared unblinkingly as she got on her hands and knees and pulled her skirt up to her waist.

Without a word she pulled her bloomers down just far enough for him to see her naked behind. She waited breathlessly for Toby to inspect her bare bottom. She flinched from his unexpected touch as he ran his hand gently over each round globe.

"See the bruises?" Bonnie asked, not able to stand the silence any longer.

"I don't see any bruises," Toby said after his careful inspection, the tightness in the crotch of his jeans making him uncomfortable. "All I see are a few pink streaks and I can barely see those."

"You're not looking close enough," Bonnie said as the wetness grew between her legs.

Toby took that opportunity to run his hands over each cheek again, squeezing the flesh between his fingers. Bonnie's soft moans encouraged him further. He pressed his clothed crotch against her backside. When Bonnie didn't protest, he unbuttoned his pants and pulled them down along with his drawers. His stiff cock sprung out towards the waiting womanhood before him.

A sudden snap and a feeling as if he'd just been stung by a wasp on his rear end grabbed his attention as he was about to make his initial thrust. If the pain didn't soften his dick, Ned Crowley mounted on his horse holding a bull whip in his hand certainly did. They were so caught up in the physical excitement that neither one heard the approaching horse.

"Damn it, you two!" Ned barked as he let the tip of his whip take another bite out of Toby's ass.

Toby scrambled to his feet pulling his pants on as quickly as he could.

"What the hell is going on?" Ned yelled as he dismounted, his eyes blazing with wrath at catching Toby about to deflower a girl he was sworn to protect.

"I…we…you see..." Toby stammered as he buttoned up his trousers.

He didn't take his eyes off the whip his boss had dangling menacingly from his hand. Toby boldly stepped between Crowley and Bonnie, who hadn't moved. She was mortified to be caught in an indecent predicament.

"Get back to those cattle," Ned said through gritted teeth. "You can expect to spend the next three days and nights out there!" he continued as he motioned for Toby to get going.

"What about her?" Toby asked, as he looked in Bonnie's direction.

"She's not your concern," Ned said steely as he began reining in the long bull whip.

Toby hesitated for a moment before leaving his boss and Bonnie alone in the field. She watched fearfully as Toby retreated. Still on all fours, she went to tug at her bloomers to cover her naked flesh. A stern word from Ned halted her movement.

"Did I give you permission to leave camp?" he asked, trying to harness his anger.

Bonnie didn't answer as tears pooled in her eyes. She knew it was useless to make an excuse to be away from camp. To be caught with a ranch hand with one's bloomers pulled down and about to do something she'd only seen farm animals do was humiliating. She remained paralyzed on all fours, her bare bottom open to the breeze…and to Ned's impending punishment.

While she was on her knees, her bottom stuck out at just the right height and angle for Ned to easily control the amount of force he would use with the whip. Not wanting to permanently injure his ward he rolled it up and squeezed one end in the palm of his large hand which left six large loops of leather dangle at the other end. An impressive punishing tool he thought as he swung back and made first contact with Bonnie's ass.

"Answer me!" Ned commanded as he swatted her backside again with the rolled up bull whip.

"Pleeessse...oooh…" Bonnie squalled as the looped layers of rawhide stung her flesh, leaving sphere shaped welts across her entire naked behind.

"Did…I…give…you…permission?" Ned asked again, punctuating each word with a hard crack to the round fleshy part of her bottom.

"Nooo," Bonnie wailed as the burning of a thousand pins seemed to be pricking deeply into her rear end.

She instinctively put one hand back to protect her backside from another barrage of painful swats. A quick flick of the leather to her palm made her change her mind as she resumed the humiliating position.

"I can't protect you," CRACK, "if you continue to disobey me," CRACK, CRACK, CRACK, Ned said as he brought the looped end across her backside over and over until Bonnie was a sobbing mess, her bottom throbbing.

"I may not be your father but I bet he would have thrashed you just as good if he caught you doing what you two were fixing to do," Ned said, his fury subsiding a little as he thanked his lucky stars he had arrived in time to save the young woman from her own naiveté.

Bonnie cried even harder when she heard his words. Her embarrassment reached new heights as she envisioned what Mr. Crowley must have witnessed when he rode in, seeing Toby rubbing up against her bare ass with that mysterious part of the male anatomy she wasn't at all familiar with. How quickly the excitement of feeling Toby's body against her own naked flesh had turned to misery. She slumped to the ground, wishing it would swallow her, unmindful that her backside was still uncovered and on display for Ned's inspection.

"I ought to horse whip that boy," Ned said as he ran his fingers through his hair in frustration.

"No, Please, NO!" Bonnie wailed. "It was entirely my fault," she declared, trying desperately to convince the trail boss.

Ned stared down at the weepy eyed girl, lying on the ground, wishing for the hundredth time he had never allowed the women to come along on the cattle drive. Completely exasperated, he yanked the girl up to stand before him.

"If I EVER catch the two of you…" he shouted as he shook her forcefully.

"You won't, I PROMISE," Bonnie pledged as fresh tears ran down her face.

Not trusting his anger, he released Bonnie and stomped toward his horse. When Bonnie was clothed Ned reached down and helped her into the saddle behind him. She stifled a groan knowing her bottom was in for a bumpy ride back to camp.

Amelia stood by the chuck wagon and spotted Bonnie and Ned ride into the camp. Turning green with envy, she watched Ned help her cousin dismount. They stood talking together and Amelia would have given anything to know what they were saying.

"I'm sorry," Bonnie said suddenly, her contriteness touching a soft spot as she stood before him.

"I mean what I said. No more running off," he warned gently as he gave her backside a quick swat. She winced but smiled shyly up at the gruff rancher.

"What…What...will…um," Bonnie started.

"Spit it out girl," Ned urged.

"What will happen to…to…Toby?" Bonnie asked hesitantly, with fear for his safety clearly written on her face.

"He'll be spending a few days and nights with the cows and away from you," Ned said, wanting to ease her anxiety a little. "You aren't to be alone with Toby or any of these cowboys," Ned said sternly as he raised Bonnie's face to look him in the eye.

"Yes sir," Bonnie said meekly.

"I can't keep you two apart but I will not tolerate you going off alone with him or any other cowboy on my drive. Do you understand?" he asked.

Bonnie shook her head. He was dumbfounded when she quickly hugged him and kissed his cheek.

"Go see if Amos needs help," he said, clearly embarrassed by the sudden display of affection.

As Bonnie walked away he looked around assuring himself that his other ward hadn't disappeared as well. He saw Amelia from a distance standing over by the wagon. He waved but Amelia turned her back and walked to the far side of the wagon out of sight. When she was sure she was alone she stomped her feet several times, outraged at witnessing the kiss between her cousin and the rancher.

"Bastard, damn no good son-of ..." Amelia gritted out between clenched teeth.

Tears welled up in her eyes as she began to devise a plan to make Ned's life miserable…or more so than usual.

\*\*\*

That evening Bonnie couldn't help but notice the cold shoulder her cousin was giving her. No matter how hard she tried to talk, Amelia would just ignore her and walk away. Bonnie needed to talk desperately. She was so confused about what almost happened between her and Toby and needed her cousin's objective advice. She missed Toby and hoped he wasn't too cold and lonely guarding the herd. She fretted about what Toby must be thinking and how he must be feeling towards her after being caught the way they were.

When the camp had settled down for the night, Amelia watched with anticipation as she saw Ned crawl into his bed roll. It didn't take him long to fold back the heavy blanket when something unexpected touched his bare feet. He frowned when he saw that a vine of poison ivy had been placed under his blanket at the foot of his sleeping spot. His first thought went to Toby but he was quickly dismissed as the culprit because the young cowpoke was out guarding the stock. He knew Bonnie didn't do it. It was clear from her continence that she didn't hold a grudge for being punished earlier. He gazed toward the chuck wagon and spotted Amelia watching him from across the camp. Their eyes locked for the briefest moment and then she looked away. The smug look on her face spoke volumes.

What the hell, he thought as he got up and used a stick to toss the offending plant into the brushes. He had half a mind to drag that hellion out of the wagon and blister her backside but he stopped himself. He was tired and rationalized that he didn't really have any proof. He would just have to keep a special eye on her.

His head began to throb as he replayed their kiss from a few days ago. It was a mistake, he reprimanded himself. He was a rancher from Texas and Amelia wanted to marry someone out west. He wasn't used to the emotions or the physical attraction she stirred in him. It wasn't easy being the boss with the responsibility of so many people and animals. He had no disillusions about himself. His gruffness was a natural part of him. He wasn't a man of many words, especially not courting words, and he had no use for public displays of affection.

In the past, if he needed a woman he usually visited a local saloon where he could get his needs met. No attachments, just a physical release. What he wanted with Amelia was private and he meant to keep it that way or not at all. With his thoughts driving him to distraction he felt like a condemned man between a rock and a hard place. With her or without her, he figured he was screwed.

***

The next morning the bottom of Ned's feet itched something fierce. He had to stop several times during the day to take his boots off and scratch his soles. Even his ankles were beginning to itch. He sought out Amos as soon as camp was set up. Amos was a godsend when it came to home remedies.

"You're the second one today. Amelia had a rash on her hands and wrists," Amos said as he pulled out a nasty smelling concoction of roots and herbs. He handed Ned a cup full of whisky.

"Drink this," Amos said as he began his four-step cure. For the second and the hardest step of all for the cook, he then poured a little whisky on the afflicted area. Amos closed his eyes, bracing himself for the torture of having to pour good whisky on the outside of the body.

"That burns like the dickens," Ned yelped as he felt the alcohol cleanse the scratched and broken skin.

"Smear this on the rash three times a day and it should be gone in a few days," the cook said as he handed Ned the smelly herbal-root remedy.

"And finally, drink another one of these," Ned was handed another cup of whisky.

"How much of this did you give Amelia," Ned asked as he peered into the cup of golden liquid.

"I didn't give her any to drink, being she's a woman and all," Amos said as he took a long swig for himself. "Don't want to catch it," he said with a wink when he noticed Ned watching him closely.

Ned shook his head and laughed to himself as he headed over to the fire. So the little brat has a rash on her hands, he thought to himself, having undoubtedly determined the guilty party. Ned decided not to confront Amelia right away. He wanted to observe her further to see what other mischief she might be up to. His itchy feet distracted him from upturning her bottom then and there, but he figured he'd get to it eventually. Ned began relishing a time in the very near future when he would have her bare bottom at his mercy.

He slept fitfully until waking suddenly from a disturbing dream. Ned laid in his bedroll staring up at the stars. His breathing returned to normal. In his dream, he had been running, searching for something. Trying to catch someone but he couldn't make out the face at first. Then Amelia's heart shaped face appeared suddenly. She was crying and calling out for him. He raced to find her.

Frustration and fear gripped him as he heard her scream. Then he was awake around a campfire, the snores of the cowboys rising and falling over the crackling of the fire. A sudden panic gripped him and he got up. Walking steadily toward the chuck wagon he heaved a heavy sigh as he saw Amelia curled up sound asleep. She looks like an angel when she sleeps, he thought. He smiled to himself at the deception, knowing the hell she could cause as his feet started itching again.

***

"Are you mad at me," Bonnie asked as she grabbed Amelia's arm the next morning before her cousin could jump down off the wagon.

Amelia stared at her cousin, not sure how to answer. Amelia couldn't get the image of Bonnie and Ned kissing out of her head. It drove her crazy to think of them together. Crazy made her do things, stupid things she wouldn't normally do. Her palms itched, she was immensely annoyed with her cousin right now and she hadn't been sleeping well. It was all Ned's fault she concluded, as she plotted more revenge against the trail boss.

"I don't want to talk about it," Amelia finally snapped, feeling a little guilty at Bonnie's crestfallen expression. "I don't care what Ned Crowley does!" she fumed to herself as she watched Bonnie climb down from the wagon looking very unhappy.

"Good morning," Ned said surprising Amelia as she refilled his coffee cup.

Breakfast had been a relaxing affair as the storm everyone had been watching the day before moved north, missing them completely.

"Get me another biscuit please," Ned requested, knowing Amelia had made them fresh that morning.

Without a word Amelia stalked over to where the biscuits were warming by the fire. She picked up two that were too close to the flame and that were badly burnt on the bottom. She carried them over to Ned.

"Have all you want," she said snidely as she dropped the burnt biscuits in his lap.

Ned didn't say a word as he picked them up and ate the tops as he watched Amelia make a hasty retreat. The cowboys looked on in silence, except for Slim.

Slim Jamison was a long time roper who was good with his hands. No one knew his real first name; everyone just called him "Slim" because of his long pointed nose. While others liked to read, smoke or play instruments, he liked to spend his spare time whittling. He was real good at carving animals, but on this particular day he had a notion to carve something new and perhaps useful. He found a piece of a board about eighteen inches long that had been discarded from a wagon train a while back. Watching the scene play out between the boss and Amelia gave him an idea for his next project.

***

"Can we please talk," Bonnie begged, as the girls sat in the wagon and the drive continued west.

"What do you want to talk about?" Amelia replied coldly.

"I need to tell you something," Bonnie said as she began to wring her hands.

"I already KNOW," Amelia said angrily.

"You do?" Bonnie's eyes grew as large as saucers, "Who told you?" she asked, clearly distressed.

"I saw you," Amelia said hatefully.

"You saw me and Toby?" Bonnie couldn't believe what she was hearing. "Oh my god, who else knows?" she asked, her eyes beginning to pool with unshed tears.

"You and TOBY?" Amelia prodded, a bit confused.

"You must HATE me," Bonnie wailed. "I didn't mean it to go that far," she sobbed into her hands.

"Wait, wait. What are you talking about?" Amelia asked, her eyebrows drawing together.

"Me and Toby. We were alone and well…he…I…showed him my bottom and…"

"And WHAT?" Amelia wanted to throttle the girl if she didn't speak up.

"Please don't be angry with me. Mr. Crowley caught us before anything really happened," Bonnie pleaded.

"You and TOBY!" Amelia squealed in delight as realization set in. She clasped her hands together and started laughing.

"What's so funny?" Bonnie asked, stunned by her cousin's laughter.

"You…Well not you exactly," she chortled. "I thought you and Ned Crowley…"

"What? That's ridiculous." Bonnie said, not believing what Amelia was implying.

"I saw the two of you ride in together and then he kissed you," Amelia accused.

"He did NOT kiss me! He took a whip to my bare ass when he caught me and Toby alone in the field," Bonnie informed.

"But I thought I saw him kiss you," Amelia said, growing happier by the second.

"I kissed him…on the CHEEK…he saved me from making a terrible mistake!" Bonnie exclaimed.

How dare he put me through all this, Amelia thought as she spied Ned urging a stray back into the herd.

"What do you think?" Bonnie asked, drawing Amelia away from her private thoughts.

"About what?" she asked.

"About what happened," Bonnie said, her exasperation showing.

"Have you talked to Toby since?" Amelia asked

"No, I haven't seen him. Mr. Crowley has him guarding the cows day and night," Bonnie replied.

"Well…I don't know what to say…Did Ned really whip your bare bottom while Toby was there?" Amelia asked.

"No, he made Toby leave before he started whipping me," Bonnie answered.

"Bonnie…" Amelia didn't know exactly how to approach her cousin with the subject. "Do you ever get a funny feeling deep down, you know, between your legs, when Ned whips you?" Amelia asked, quickly hiding her face in her hands from embarrassment.

"What kind of funny feeling?" Bonnie asked innocently. "The only feeling I get is a fiery feeling on my ass," she admitted.

"Never mind," Amelia said quickly, wanting to change the subject.

"I will tell you a secret though," Bonnie whispered as Amelia's head popped up. "I don't think I would mind at all if Toby was taking me over his knee and spanking my bare bottom," she said with a gleam in her eye. "Sometimes I dream it is Toby punishing me and I feel all warm inside. Do you think I'm wicked?" Bonnie asked hesitantly.

"No, I don't think you're wicked at all," Amelia said as she gave her cousin a reassuring hug.

# THORN IN HIS BOOT

## Chapter 5

By the fourth week of the cattle drive, Ned Crowley and his cowboys had fallen into a good routine. So far they only had a few setbacks on their trek west. Each delay was the direct result of the two young women accompanying the drive. If Ned had known the trouble Amelia and Bonnie would cause, he would have left them in Texas, regardless of their sob story about fleeing arranged marriages and his cook's broken arm.

Ned watched Amelia as she walked around pouring coffee for his men. He swirled around his untouched drink as he pondered his latest problem. She had been especially prickly of late. The poison ivy in his bed roll had undoubtedly been her idea. It took great restraint on his part to keep from upturning her bottom and giving her a whipping she wouldn't soon forget when he found out it was her. He knew she was still up to something by the way she would watch him anytime he was around. Her sweet disposition this evening when she served him supper confirmed his suspicions. The smile, although welcomed, was a complete turnaround from her recent demeanor and it puzzled him to no end.

He absently scratched his ankle as he continued to watch the little hellion. She had been angry for days but he couldn't for the life of him think of why her feathers were all ruffled. Sure, he'd lashed her ass when she got into mischief but she had been forewarned when she took the job that any disobedience would be dealt with severely. But recently she had become rude and belligerent; two things Ned couldn't abide by.

Amelia noticed the camaraderie between the trail boss and his cowboys. For a second she regretted her plan. She knew she was pushing Ned with each prank but she didn't know how to react to his recent coldness. He'd spank the daylights out of her bare backside and kiss her one minute and then be distant and cold the next. Recently he began ignoring her altogether.

Let's see if this gets your attention, she thought earlier, as she poured an inch of salt into one particular cup before filling it with coffee. As she walked around refilling mugs she watched and waited for Ned to take his first sip.

The sound of spewing liquid was unmistakable as the rancher spit the vile salt laden coffee into the fire. He glared in Amelia's direction. She gave him her most innocent look as he threw the remainder of the nasty coffee over his shoulder. The cowhands looked on silently, as they felt the tension between the boss and Amelia.

Ned got to his feet suddenly and walked toward her. The grim determination was evident on his rugged face. A few snickers could be heard around the campfire. Slim Jamison shook his head and kept on whittling.

Amelia's stomach began doing flip flops when he stopped in front of her. To her bewilderment and frustration instead of confronting her, he held out his mug and requested a refill. Without a word he walked back to his seat and began talking with Slim. Every now and then Ned would slide his gaze in Amelia's direction noticing her sour expression had returned.

✷✷✷

"OUCH!" Ned hollered early the next morning as he finished pulling his boot on and stood up.

Quickly he took it off and peered inside. The pain to his heel throbbed as he shook out the boot. A handful of thorns fell to the ground at his feet. He picked one up and studied it intently as he sighed heavily. He just caught a glimpse of Amelia ducking down in the chuck wagon. Rubbing his sore heel he replaced his boot and limped over to saddle his horse. He spent the rest of the day while herding cattle thinking up a hundred ways in which to turn the little lady's backside three shades of purple.

*\*\*\**

That evening, as the girls were collecting firewood, Bonnie came across a red ant hill. Bonnie's unexpected yelp brought her cousin running when a tiny fire ant bit her finger. The two watched the red bugs running around on the ground this way, then that. It gave Amelia an idea.

"We better get this firewood to Amos," Bonnie said as she held her armload of wood.

"You go on, I have a few more pieces to collect," Amelia said as she watched Bonnie walk the few yards back to camp.

Amelia took a dead branch and laid it over the ant hill. She watched as the ants scaled it. When it looked like enough had climbed on, she carefully picked up the stick and hastily walked toward the fire. With a mischievous look in her eye, she laid the stick livened with ants next to Ned's bedroll.

Amelia was brimming with excitement as she waited to see Ned's reaction later that evening.

"Watch this," she said to Bonnie as they were about to climb in the chuck wagon.

Bonnie looked in the direction Amelia indicated. The cowboys were bedding down for the night.

"What am I looking for," Bonnie asked, confused by her cousin's recent manner.

"Just watch and see," Amelia said, trying to hide a giggle.

It didn't take long for movement to be seen coming from Ned's blanket. First it was a single jerk as one ant bit him on his forearm. By the time he flung off his covers, several dozen had attacked him leaving a fiery trail of pain on his arms and legs. He danced around trying to wipe the bugs off as they continued to bite. He shook out his bedroll and knocked off the last remaining ants before he turned in the direction of the chuck wagon. Amelia was laughing so hard she had to turn her back. Bonnie was shocked and looked at her cousin reproachfully.

"What did you do?" Bonnie asked, stunned at her cousin's behavior.

"A little ants in his pants," Amelia said through her laughter.

"Why?" Bonnie asked as she climbed into the wagon.

"Because he ignores me!" Amelia said a bit childishly.

Her laughter was quickly replaced by brooding when she saw that Ned wasn't taking the bait. He moved his bedroll to another spot around the campfire and lay down. It brought a smile to his lips when he caught Amelia stomping her feet in aggravation just before she climbed into the wagon.

Amelia had a fitful night's sleep. She tossed and turned as she dreamed she was being swallowed by an ant hill. She winced at the tiny stings all over her body. Suddenly the stinging was concentrated to only her backside. She wiggled her bottom trying to dislodge the ants that had accumulated on her bare cheeks. Her flesh had turned red as each globe was covered in the fiery ants. As she continued to dream, the ants fell away but to her dismay her bottom remained red. The stinging became sharper. She was staring at the ground with her bottom turned up as she found herself over her father's knee. She felt the sharp crack of his belt as he brought it down on her buttocks again and again. She began to cry and pleaded for him to stop. Suddenly his face was gone and Ned's appeared in its place. The rancher was now holding her and kissing her lips. She could feel his hands roaming all over her body. She was completely naked standing before him. A tingly sensation between her legs began to build. A moan escaped her lips as he touched her breasts. His thumb and index finger rubbing each nipple until they were hard. His hands, rough with calluses, parted her thighs. His lips curled as she groaned at his intimate touch. Suddenly an ant appeared on his face. His smile turned cruel as he squeezed and pinched her bare ass cheeks. She could taste the salt from her tears as they ran down her face. Amelia was pushed backward abruptly. Ned turned his back to her and walked away. She called after him but he ignored her cries. As she ran to catch up with him, she felt the poison ivy vines wrap around her arms and legs. Her skin turned green, her body faded into the vine as if she were a chameleon. Ned will never find me, she thought as she woke with a start.

Amelia breathed deeply, relief flooding over her at the realization it was only a dream. She stared up at the stars twinkling overhead. The only sounds were that of a screeching owl and the snores of Amos sleeping soundly under the wagon. She peered over the rim of the wagon and saw Ned asleep by the other cowboys. She recognized his frame easily amongst the dozen or so men snoozing around the fire. She stared at his sleeping form as a tingling sensation began to build in her middle. She laid back down in the wagon and rolled onto her side away from her cousin. Amelia began to replay the memory of their kiss the last time she and Ned were alone together. She felt the wetness between her legs as she envisioned him leading her deep into the forest away from the others. He ordered her to undress as he silently watched her. She put a hand under her bloomers and ran it down her stomach to the juncture of her legs as she continued to fantasize. Her fingers sought out her clit and she rubbed it with a slow circular motion. She remembered his tanned muscular body. He was taking off his belt. Her breathing quickened; the exhilaration building to unbelievable heights. She rubbed a firm ass cheek with her other hand as she imagined him bending her over a log. The first slap of his belt brought a groan to her lips as she continued to rub her clit. The tension in her body mounted with each flick of her nub. She squeezed her fleshy cheek firmly as she envisioned another crack of the leather. With each swat of the belt her body became inflamed until she reached her peek and her juices made a puddle in her bloomers.

***

The next morning she was roughly awakened by Bonnie. She could hear Amos hollering for help with making breakfast.

"Get UP!" Bonnie shoved hard trying to move Amelia off the blankets.

Bonnie wasn't pleased with her cousin. She didn't like the way Amelia had been acting the last few days. Her snide remarks toward the trail boss and her overall insolence were getting on Bonnie's nerves. Amelia's stunt last night with the ants was the last straw. She couldn't figure out why Amelia was acting that way; but she noticed her vindictiveness seemed to be aimed at Ned Crowley.

Bonnie didn't want to get into any more trouble and was afraid that was exactly where her cousin was headed. She just hoped Amelia didn't drag her along. It wouldn't be the first time they stood side by side waiting to get a thrashing. It had been a few days since Ned had whipped either of them and Bonnie hoped she would never give him another reason to bare her bottom and punish her. She had been trying so hard to be obedient and respectful, even to old Amos who seemed to make it his mission to find fault with her work. She found herself biting her tongue on more than one occasion after unfair remarks had been made toward her. She was afraid she would end up turned over Ned's knee on the receiving end of his leather belt.

It had been several days since Bonnie had seen Toby. Not since they'd been caught almost making love in the field. Even though Ned assured her the cowboy's only punishment would be extra long shifts with the cattle, she worried that the trail boss might change his mind and whip her true love. To add to her suffering, when Toby came into the camp last night she couldn't help but notice he purposefully kept his distance from her. Her heart sank, thinking Toby no longer wanted to be with her.

Bonnie tried to keep her distance from Amelia while they worked to prepare the morning meal. Her temper boiled over when Amelia dropped the oatmeal spoon and the sticky oats splattered all over the front of Bonnie's dress. Amelia began to laugh at the astonished face her cousin made as she stood by the large kettle covered in the gooey mess. Bonnie's face reddened as the cowpokes joined in the laughter. Reaching into the lukewarm pot Bonnie brought out a handful of oats and threw it at Amelia. Her cousin's face and hair now matched Bonnie's dress.

"You did THAT on PURPOSE!" Amelia shrieked as the cowboy's hardy laughter could be heard behind her.

Amelia wiped the oatmeal from her face and slung the remnants at her cousin. Amos rolled his eyes as the two girls yelled at each other. Bonnie shoved her cousin backward, making her fall to the ground. The spectators got quiet when Amelia jumped up and slapped Bonnie across the face, leaving a glowing handprint on her cheek. In the blink of an eye the girls were pulling each other's hair and wrestling on the ground. Ned and Toby ran over and yanked the two women apart. Toby helped Bonnie to her feet while Ned hoisted Amelia up. Amelia made a sudden lunge at her cousin. Ned held her fast around the waist holding her back.

"That's ENOUGH!" Ned's terse voice could be heard throughout the entire camp.

Amelia, heedless of his words, kept reaching in Bonnie's direction until a hard swat to her behind got her attention.

"What's this all about?" Ned demanded to know as he looked from Amelia to Bonnie.

Amelia was heaving from the exertion, madder than hell. Bonnie began to cry as she touched her red cheek with her finger tips. Toby put his arm around her shoulders comfortingly as she whimpered softly.

"I can tell ya," Amos spoke up. "That one there…" he said as he pointed toward Amelia, "got gruel on that other one and the next thing ya know she hit her and there ya have it. They were rolling around on the ground til you two come and broke them up," Amos finished with an exasperated sigh.

Ned rolled his eyes, wondering what he had done to deserve the tribulations brought on by these two women. He instructed Toby to saddle two extra horses for today's ride.

"No easy wagon ride for either of ya today," Ned announced, "Now go wash off that mess."

As Bonnie turned to leave he stopped her to examine her cheek, relieved no permanent damage had been done.

***

Later, after returning a wandering calf to its mother, Ned rode up to the chuck wagon Amos was driving. He didn't say anything for a long time as he watched the two women riding on horseback ahead of him. Each took up opposite sides of the herd, staying as far away from each other as they possibly could.

"My arms about healed. Ya could leave them at the next town," Amos said as he watched his trail boss closely.

"I could," Ned said with a grim frown as he urged his horse into a gallop.

Amos chuckled to himself as he watched his boss ride away; glad he wasn't in Ned's shoes.

The gossip that the trail boss was dumping the girls at the next town spread like wildfire. Toby's face was grim when he rode up to Bonnie's horse to relay the news.

"I hear the Boss is thinking about leaving you and your cousin at the next town," he said in a flat tone.

"Oh NO! He wouldn't really leave us, would he? I know we've caused a…a...little inconvenience…

but he wouldn't really abandon us..." she said as tears pooled in her eyes.

"INCONVENIENCE? I don't think the trouble you girls have caused is a *little* anything, let alone an *inconvenience*. Downright difficult and aggravating would be more like it." Toby took his hat off and wiped the sweat from his brow before giving Bonnie a good-naturedly grin.

"Don't worry, things will work out," he said reassuringly as he galloped off.

"I don't want to talk to YOU!" Amelia said when Bonnie rode up next to her.

"Ned plans on leaving us at the next town," Bonnie said sharply.

"What? He can't do that!" Amelia protested, not believing what she had just heard.

"It's true. Toby just told me. Maybe we could talk to Mr. Crowley," Bonnie suggested hesitantly.

✳✳✳

That night, as everyone was finishing supper, Amos found Bonnie crying on the backside of a tree just on the outskirts of the camp. Her gut wrenching sobs got to old Amos. Against his better judgment, he asked what was ailing her. She threw her arms around his neck and wept into his shoulder. It irritated Amos that this weepy woman touched a soft place in his heart.

"No need to cry, it can't be all that bad. What seems to be the trouble?" Amos asked as he awkwardly patted her back.

"He...He..."

"He WHAT? Is it TOBY? Did he do something to ya? Why I'll whip him so hard..." Amos got angry jumping to conclusions and thinking the worst. The protectiveness he suddenly felt for the tearful girl surprised him.

"No, no it's not Toby," sniffled Bonnie.

"He who? You're not making sense girl," he said.

"It's Ned. He is going to...to... ABANDON us at the next town," she wailed. Amos patted her shoulder, beginning to understand the reason behind her distress.

"Go clean the dishes and let old Amos take care of it," he said as he guided her toward the camp.

The two girls were very quiet that evening, neither one speaking to anyone or each other. Since everyone had heard the gossip, no one felt much like talking. Except for the scraping of Slim's whittling knife, it was very quiet around the campfire.

***

The next morning Bonnie hesitantly approached Ned just as he mounted his horse.

"Please don't send us away. If we promise to be EXTRA good can we stay on?" she blurted out, her eyes brimming with tears.

Ned looked down at the girl and shook his head. His face was void of any emotion.

"Darlin, being good just ain't your strong point, especially for that cousin of yours," replied Ned.

"But…there must be something we could do," she pleaded.

"I'll think about it," he said before riding away.

After several hours of riding in the wagon, Amelia's curiosity got the better of her.

"So what did he say?" Amelia asked.

"He said he'd think about it," answered Bonnie.

"That's the same as saying no," Amelia pouted.

"Oh, what are we going to do?" Bonnie wrung her hands.

"We'll find another cattle drive or wagon train… something," Amelia said.

"But we don't have money to join a wagon train," Bonnie stated bluntly.

"Stop pestering me. I'll think of something," Amelia said irritably.

It hurt a lot that Ned seemed to care so little; that he would just leave them in some old dirty town.

"That bastard," she mumbled.

Amos heard their conversation and a sly smile crossed his lips. They would soon be coming to the town of *Oakleaf*. It's a rough town, no place for decent girls, he thought. Ned was a good man and Amos couldn't imagine the boss leaving the girls in that cesspool of gamblers and scoundrels. But just to be sure…

***

Ned found a large clearing a mile outside of *Oakleaf* to rest the herd for the night. He had been preoccupied with the problem of what to do with the girls all day. No solution satisfied him. Damned if he did and damned if he didn't. Amos's hollering got his attention.

"OHHHH my ARM! my ARM!" Amos was yelling.

His recently healed arm was caught in the wagon wheel. The spokes pinned it at an unnatural angle against the axle. The girls were jumping down off the wagon to help when Ned rode up, reining his horse in hastily. The trail boss helped get the old cook loose, ordering the girls to get some blankets and water.

"Luckily it does not seem to be broken," Ned said after careful inspection.

"Oh Boss, it hurts, it really hurts, I need my sling," Amos said holding his arm and wailing like a banshee.

"Get him his sling," he barked at Toby, who had just ridden up.

"And some whisky," Amos added with a shout.

Ned set his hat on the edge of the wagon and ran his hands through his hair, thankful the injury was no worse than it was. He was a little shaken, thinking how close his cook could have come to losing his arm altogether. He went to help as Amos tried to tie the sling around his neck. Using his good arm, Amos snatched the whisky bottle from Toby and took a long swig. He then offered it to Ned who looked like he could use a nip himself.

After they had made Amos as comfortable as possible, the girls stood by the wagon dejectedly. They had been gathering and packing their belongings while riding in the wagon all day. As the men came into camp, a crowd gathered around Amos. Amelia climbed up and sat down on the edge of the wagon to get a better view of what was happening.

"Boss, I hate it terribly, seeing how you want to get rid of them girls and all, but I ain't gonna be able to do all the cooking and stuff that needs doing around here without some help. This old arm just ain't gonna be much use to me for awhile," Amos said sorrowfully.

Ned took another swig from the bottle. He felt it burn all the way down to his stomach. He looked at Amos, then to Toby and finally to the disheartened women.

"They can stay," he said shaking his head, damning his luck to hell.

Toby gave a whoop and a holler as he picked up Bonnie and twirled her around. Her eyes were brimming with tears. As soon as Toby put her back on her feet she ran up to Ned and gave him a big hug. Ned turned red with embarrassment.

"Don't forget," he said sternly, "you promised to be EXTRA good."

Some of the cowboys laughed and some cheered. Amelia watched Ned, wishing he would grab her and twirl her around.

"Hey, has anybody seen my hat?" Ned asked.

Everyone started looking around on the ground and by the horses. Amelia felt something under her behind as she shifted on the wagon's edge. She lifted one cheek and pulled out a beaver colored Stetson.

"Oh!" she gasped, as every eye turned toward her, holding up the flattened hat with a grimace.

"My HAT!" Ned yelled as he stomped toward Amelia.

She handed him his crushed hat and shrugged her shoulders innocently. To her surprise, Ned grabbed her by the arm and began dragging her toward the far side of the wagon. Slim stepped in their path.

"Get outta my way Slim," Ned said tersely, his patience completely gone.

"I just thought you might want this," Slim said as he handed Ned the wood he had been whittling on the last few days.

It was a paddle. Eighteen inches long, six inches wide and a good inch thick with a sturdy handle. Slim had carved the girls' names on it along with a few holes to help it pass through the air before coming in contact with a bare bottom.

"Thanks," Ned said as he took the paddle and marched Amelia out of sight.

Ned found a stump and sat down pulling Amelia over his lap. He promptly hiked up her skirt and pulled her drawers down to her knees. Amelia struggled, half heartily remembering all the pranks she had pulled the last couple of days. Ned positioned Amelia's bare bottom high on one knee, using his other leg to secure her legs in place. Her hands rested on the ground balancing her body over his knee. The loud crack of the paddle startled her as the slow burn began to seep through her cheeks.

"Poison ivy in my bed…" CRACK, CRACK, CRACK, the paddle rained down so fast she didn't have time to catch her breath. "…thorns in my boot…" CRACK, CRACK, CRACK, CRACK "…and fire ants in my bed," he said as he gave her bare cheeks several more hard whacks with the paddle, remembering the bites on his arms and legs.

Amelia was sobbing, her fanny was on fire, and Ned didn't seem close to being done with punishing her bare flesh.

"Salt in my coffee, not to mention mangling my hat," WHACK, WHACK, WHACK, WHACK, WHACK, CRACK, Ned continued.

"And…" SMACK, SMACK "you've been…" SMACK "a discourteous…" SMACK, SMACK SMACK, "and EXTREMELY annoying…" CRACK, CRACK, "little girl," WHACK, WHACK, WHACK.

"Pleeease, I'mmm SOOORRRY!" Amelia wailed as she struggled to get off his lap.

Ned paid no attention to her plea as he continued to bombard her fanny with the unyielding wooden paddle. She could feel her ass jiggle with each stroke.

Wiggling her behind only made Ned raise her bottom higher, leaving her sit spot wide open as the paddle found new territory for his administrations.

Her wails turned to sobs as she lay completely submissive to his punishment. Seeing her resistance fade, Ned slowed his swats down considerably until he stopped all together. Amelia's bottom glowed with a bright red blush. Each rounded globe ached and throbbed as she lay across his lap, too exhausted to rise. Ned put the paddle down on the ground next to him. He began rubbing her bare cheeks, allowing Amelia time to regain her composure.

"No more pranks, ya hear?" Ned asked as he continued to rub her fanny.

"Yesss siiirrr," Amelia replied, suddenly aware of the tender touch of his callused hand on her naked flesh.

"No more bad temper or sour looks," Ned demanded.

"No more of that sir," she said, feeling the tingling in her middle.

"Promise to be EXTRA GOOD," he said, giving her naked bottom a sharp swat with his hand.

"I promise," she said meekly, feeling the wetness between her legs.

To Amelia's disappointment, Ned helped her off of his lap.

"My bottom must be three shades of purple," she said shyly as she pulled up her bloomers, wincing as the material touched her swollen bottom.

"When you can finally sit down, sit on a rolled up blanket…anything besides my HAT," he said sternly.

He really cares, she thought, smiling to herself as she reached up and kissed him full on the mouth before hurrying off toward the fire. What in the hell am I going to do with that little lady, Ned wondered as he sat on the stump for several minutes. It suddenly dawned on him that all those pranks were just a cry for his attention. All she needs is a good thrashing, he thought. He wondered if that will be a daily occurrence with her. He couldn't believe how close he'd come to letting her go today, leaving her in some seedy town. How am I gonna let her go at the end of the trail, he wondered miserably.

The next morning Ned watched as Amos hoisted the heavy kettle up into the wagon using both his arms.

A smile creased Ned's face as he chuckled to himself, "You sly old coot."

# THE OUTLAWS

## Chapter 6

"OUT!" the sheriff of *Oakleaf* barked as he unlocked and opened the jail cell door.

The two cowboys, Carl and Grady, grabbed their hats and walked over to the sheriff's desk. They picked up their gun belts and put them on as they made their way toward the door leading to the street of the old dilapidated town.

"UHHHM, aren't you boys forgetting something?" the sheriff asked, clearing his throat. "That was twenty dollars or twenty more days," he said as he held out his hand.

The cowboys stopped in their tracks and turned around to face the crooked old sheriff. Carl reached into his shirt pocket and handed the sheriff the money.

"EACH!" the sheriff said as he counted only twenty dollars.

"It don't pay to be too greedy," Carl sneered as he pulled out his pistol and loaded cartridges into the empty chambers.

The sheriff held up his hands as he eyed Carl's revolver. He had recognized the scoundrels from the *WANTED* posters when he arrested the pair a few hours before. Cattle rustling and theft were only a few of their crimes. The sheriff couldn't collect the bounty, so he would release them if they paid a fine.

### ✳✳✳

The rain started just as Amelia and her cousin, Bonnie, got the canvas over the wagon. It would be a slow, muddy trudge. Sometimes the rain came in sheets so hard Amos couldn't see five feet in front of the horses as he drove the chuck wagon. The rain made it hard to ride, let alone keep an eye on the cattle that wandered off.

Ned stopped the drive a few hours after leaving the outskirts of *Oakleaf*. The mud made it too dangerous for the horses and the wagon. Having to spend time rounding up the strays is better than a horse going lame or worse, Ned thought as he gave the signal to stop.

Most of the men headed for shelter under a large stand of trees, while a few unfortunate ones rode guard over the cattle.

The rain let up just before dark. Amos and the girls hurried to get supper ready as they rounded up the few scant pieces of dry firewood they could find. By nine, the dishes were done and everyone was sitting around the fire. Slim was telling one of his ghost stories as they all drank coffee and listened intently. The girls were hanging on every word, wondering if there truly were spirits walking the earth at night waiting to snatch up some unsuspecting prospector or lost maiden.

"Hello, in the camp," a deep voice said, making everyone jumped and the girls scream. "Coffee smells good, can we sit a spell?" the voice asked.

Ned motioned for the two cowboys to come closer so he could get a good look at them. He instantly noticed the guns around their waist. After a wave from Ned, Amos poured a couple of mugs of hot coffee for the strangers.

Amelia and Bonnie watched as the firelight played across the two handsome visitors' faces. The girls giggled when the men winked in their direction before taking a seat closest to the trail boss. The girls couldn't hear what they were saying to Ned but they were shaking hands as it seemed an agreement had been made. The newcomers introduced themselves to the cousins before making up their bed roll.

"Good evening ladies," Carl said as he tipped his hat. "I'm Carl and this is my brother, Grady."

"That's Amelia and her cousin, Bonnie," Ned said as he stepped forward, surprising everyone. "These ladies help with the cooking and nothing more," Ned said as he eyed his newest trail hands steadily, making sure they each understood his "hands off" message.

"By the way, if you're gonna work for me, no guns allowed," Ned said as he pointed at their holsters. "Amos will hold them for ya."

Grady gave his brother a sideways look before unbuckling his belt and handed over his gun to the cook. Carl did the same, not taking his eyes off the rancher.

"Ya'll get some sleep. We'll be pulling out early tomorrow," Ned announced as he watched Carl and Grady head off to bed down.

He didn't like the looks Bonnie and Amelia were giving the new cowhands. He could hear their girlish giggles all the way from the wagon.

"Keep an eye out," Ned said in a low voice to Amos as he refilled his coffee cup for the last time.

Amos nodded with understanding before going to unroll his bed beneath the wagon.

***

Carl watched as Amelia headed off into the woods in search of firewood. She hadn't gone too far when, as if stalking her, the cowboy appeared from behind a tree giving her a fright.

"You scared me!" she exclaimed dropping her firewood and clutching her hand to her chest.

"Beg your pardon miss," Carl said with a sly grin while his eyes roamed up and down her body, making Amelia blush slightly.

"I know where there is some dryer wood," he said, watching the woman closely.

"And where might that be," she responded saucily, trying not to be too obvious with her flirting.

"Out a piece, I saw some in a cave, last night," Carl answered.

"But it was dark," Amelia pointed out.

"I have good eyesight," Carl said smoothly as he turned and walked deeper into the woods.

Amelia watched his retreating steps before quickly running to catch up with him.

✳✳✳

"We've gone too far from camp," Amelia sighed as she looked around completely lost, not sure what direction camp was in. "I don't want to get into trouble."

Her bottom tingled as she thought about the spanking she'd gotten the last time she left camp without permission. Ned would certainly tan her hide if she didn't get back.

"Come on Amelia, no one will know," Carl said as he tugged at her hand. "The firewood ain't much further," he said, trying to persuade her to follow him a little farther into the forest.

Upon the mention of the firewood she relented. Ned couldn't possibly get angry, I'm only gathering firewood as instructed, she rationalized, following Carl farther away from camp.

"Ouch!" Carl exclaimed as he stumbled to the ground. He sat up and reached for his ankle.

"Are you alright?" Amelia asked worriedly as she knelt down beside him.

His kiss was so quick it caught Amelia by surprise. She felt the tightness in her middle as she watched Carl intently. He kissed her again more forcefully. With their lips still locked together, his hands went around her waist urging her closer to his body. She giggled as he ran his hands up and down her sides. Her nervous laughter stopped suddenly as his fingers brushed the sides of her breasts. She pulled away only to be roughly yanked toward him. One hand grabbed her left breast and squeezed hard while his other hand held her fast with an iron grip to her forearm. His forcefulness ignited something within Amelia. Soon she was molded to his body. She felt a hand on her knee pulling up the material of her dress. She envisioned it was Ned instead of Carl rubbing her breast and placing his hand under her skirt.

"AMELIA!" she heard her name.

The voice, as if conjured from her fantasy, belonged to Ned. He could see the young woman sitting on the ground in an embrace with his new hired hand. His temper flared as he ordered Carl back to camp.

"But his ankle," Amelia said, trying to explain.

Astonishment crossed her face as Carl jumped up and quickly headed back to camp without a word to Ned or Amelia. Her eyes widened as she sat on the ground and watched the trail boss begin taking his belt off.

He didn't have to say a word as she forced herself to stand. With knees knocking she stood before the angry man. He yanked her around to face a large tree trunk. She braced herself against the tree with both hands as tears began to spill down her face.

"I was just getting firewood," Amelia stated defiantly, finding his treatment of her completely unfair.

Ned gave her clothed behind a good smack as he positioned her bottom out farther from the tree. He didn't say anything as he raised her skirt and tucked it around her waist. He reached out and with one tug had her bloomers down around her knees, revealing her firm round globes. He noticed they were still pink from the whipping he'd given her the other day. His mind went back to the last time he bared her bottom and paddled her soundly for all the pranks she pulled. He recalled the kiss she gave him moments after her chastisement.

He was brought back to the present as the bare bottom began to wiggle. His silence stretching her nerves, Amelia began to fidget. She was growing tired of waiting for him to begin the punishment.

The first crack of his belt across her rump made Amelia jump. She felt the fire as the leather left a searing red welt across both her ass cheeks. Ned rained the thick leather down on her bottom again and again, trying to wipe out the image of Amelia wrapped tightly in Carl's arms in an intimate embrace.

"Did I give you permission to be out here?" he finally asked as he slowed his strikes.

"NO, but I..." Amelia began to answer.

CRACK, CRACK, CRACK, three more swats of the belt rained down before she could finish.

"Did I give you permission to be out here?" Ned repeated, CRACK, WHACK, CRACK.

"I was getting firewooood," she tried to explain just as three more hard licks of the belt were felt.

"Did I…" CRACK, "give you…" CRACK, "permission…" CRACK,CRACK, "to be out here?" CRACK, CRACK, WHACK Ned asked for the third time, his patience wearing thin.

"Nooo sirrr," Amelia finally said meekly through her sobs.

"Did I give you permission to be alone with that man?" Not waiting for an answer, Ned leathered her backside a dozen times before stopping for an answer.

"Nooo, sssiiirrr," Amelia groaned, lifting one foot off the ground as the last particularly hard strike bounced off her glowing red bottom.

Ned continued to lay the belt to her ass cheeks several more times. When he finished, he abruptly yanked up her bloomers and snatched her by the arm, leading her silently to camp. He didn't say a word as she glared at his back. She refused to speak to him at all. Amelia thought that he was being completely unfair, although she didn't have a single stick of firewood to give her excuse an ounce of credibility.

***

"Where have you been?" Bonnie asked when Amelia reached the kettle she was stirring.

"That damn Ned!" she ground out through gritted teeth as she slammed the coffee percolator onto the iron grate.

"What did you do?" Bonnie asked with a sigh, knowing her cousin all too well.

"I went to get firewood and he WHIPPED ME for NO REASON!" Amelia said indignantly.

"He didn't do that…" Bonnie said with doubt.

"Oh yes he DID!" Amelia spat out, grabbing Bonnie by the hand and pulling her to the far side of the wagon. "Look, see the welts?" she asked as she lifted her skirt and pulled her bloomers down just to the tops of her thighs.

Bonnie peered at her cousin's backside and grimaced at the angry welts across her rear end.

"Does it hurt much?" Bonnie asked as Amelia adjusted her clothes.

"Hell yes it hurts…and I didn't even do ANYTHING," she said, purposefully forgetting to mention Carl's part in the reason she was punished.

"Guess what?" Bonnie asked excitedly, trying to distract her cousin. "I think that cowboy…ya know…Grady…I think he likes me," she whispered.

Amelia stared at her cousin questioningly, "What about Toby?" she asked.

"Can't I have two men like me?" Bonnie asked with a giggle as they walked back to the cooking grates.

***

Amelia gave steely looks at Ned all morning. Her gaze searched around for Carl. He must be out collecting strays, she thought as she rode in the wagon. Bonnie droned on and on about Grady while they jostled along. Amelia's head began to pound, matching the throbbing of her backside, as the wagon bumped its wheels over rocks and ruts.

"...and his hand accidently brushed against my…" Bonnie babbled.

"What?" Amelia questioned, all of her attention suddenly drawn toward her cousin, catching a few of Bonnie's words.

"Grady touched me on my…" Bonnie began giggling again.

"ON YOUR WHAT?" Toby asked in a booming voice from the side of the wagon.

Both girls turned in surprise to see the cowboy riding alongside. Bonnie was clearly startled by Toby's sudden appearance at a most unfortunate time and during a most private conversation. When it was evident that Bonnie wasn't going to say anymore, Toby cussed to himself and quickly rode away.

"Do you think he's mad?" Bonnie asked sheepishly.

"Who cares," Amelia said bitterly as she spied Ned on his horse about fifty yards away.

### ✻✻✻

"Please take us with you," Amelia begged Carl as she held the reins of his horse after supper that night. She looked around anxiously hoping no one would see and try to stop them.

"Alright, up you go," Carl said giving her body an appraising looking.

He reached down and helped Amelia up behind him. She can repay me with her luscious body later tonight, he thought. Her leg bumped into the bulging saddle bag causing the flap to come open.

Bonnie settled in behind Grady as the four made their way through the thick underbrush at the base of the rocky hill. Amelia was so angry with Ned. When she saw the two cowboys leaving the trail she made a rash decision and talked Bonnie into leaving the cattle drive.

"What will Mr. Crowley say?" Bonnie had asked anxiously.

"He can go to hell!" Amelia said vehemently, her bottom still stinging from his punishment.

Amelia wished she hadn't made such a hasty decision as they rode further away from the camp. Some of her anger dissipated as she hung on to Carl's waist to keep from falling off his horse.

When they stopped for the night, Carl ordered her to unsaddle his horse as he gave her rump a resounding smack. The cruel grin on his face was unmistakable.

  Bonnie was instructed to do the same but not before Grady lifted her skirt to get an eye full of her bloomers. Outraged, she swatted his hand away angrily. Grady slapped her hard across the face. She whimpered as she tried to unsaddle the horse. The girls' fear mounted as they overheard the outlaws' conversation.

  "Which one do you want?" Grady asked.

  "I get her first," Carl said sneering in Amelia's direction. "And you can have the other one."

  "Then can we switch?" Grady asked excitedly as his pecker throbbed in his pants.

  "Sure, why not," he answered, with a wicked grin.

  Carl envisioned taking Amelia for the first time. He felt the leather of his belt between his fingers as he wondered what it would be like to beat her naked flesh as he plunged into her from behind. His cock began to press against his trousers.

  Bonnie yelped as the saddle fell to the ground, catching Grady's attention. He quickly walked over and slapped Bonnie again for her carelessness. As he went to take off his belt, Amelia rushed over and placed a gentle hand on Grady's arm. She gave him a sly smile and offered to take care of the saddle. Momentarily distracted by things to come, Grady pinched her backside and joined his brother by the fire. Bonnie breathed a sigh of relief as Amelia pulled her over to Carl's horse. His saddle bag was open and Amelia pointed to what was inside. Bonnie gasped when she saw a revolver and a wad of cash.

"That's Ned's," Amelia whispered, recognizing the items from the strong box that Amos kept under the wagon seat.

"I wish Toby was here," Bonnie said as she started to cry.

"We can't wait," Amelia said as she wished Ned was there, not caring how hard he would punish her this time for running off.

✳✳✳

"Boss, the guns and money are gone," Amos said to Ned later that evening.

"Damn it!" Crowley swore.

"Must have happened when I went to the bushes last night, that chili kept me away from camp longer than I like," Amos said shamefully.

"Are any cowpokes missing?" the trail boss asked as he looked around the campfire.

"Just those two new ones, maybe it's their turn to guard tonight," Amos offered.

"No, Slim is riding herd tonight," Ned said. "Where are the girls?" he asked suspiciously as he peered into the chuck wagon.

"Thought they went to bed," Amos replied.

"Damn it, they're gone too! Get some men together!" he ordered as he went to saddle his horse.

***

"You women get over here, it's time to pay for your passage," Carl said, his meaning very clear to both girls as they stood shivering by the horses.

Grady grabbed Bonnie by the arm and drug her toward his bedroll. She screamed and tried to pull away until a hard blow to her face sent her reeling to the ground by the fire. The two men laughed harshly as Grady began to unbutton his pants. The look of terror on Bonnie's face could be seen clearly by the firelight.

Not knowing what to do, Amelia grabbed the pistol from the saddle bag and pointed it at Grady.

"LET HER BE!" Amelia said, her voice as cold as ice.

She didn't know if it was loaded. Betting it was too dark for the outlaws to tell, she kept it aimed at Grady's middle, praying the men wouldn't call her bluff. Grady stared at the gun and backed slowly away from Bonnie.  Bonnie jumped up and ran behind her cousin.

"Now you ain't gonna shoot us," Carl said looking Amelia in the eye trying to determine if she had it in her to pull the trigger.

"No but I will!" a thunderous voice was heard behind the girls. "Give me the gun," Ned said steadily as he eased behind Amelia and took the revolver out of her shaky hands.

Carl made a slight move for the gun on his side but thought better of it when a blast from Amos' rifle splattered dirt on his boot.

"Drop them guns," Ned's steely voice rang with authority.

Carl and Grady quickly unbuckled their gun belts and let them slide to the ground seeing they were completely surrounded by a dozen cowboys. It was Toby who threw the first punch knocking out three of Grady's teeth.

※※※

Ned led the girls down a narrow footpath to a clearing where he had built a fire earlier. He made the girls sit on a fallen log.

He sat on a stump and began tearing apart an old horse bridal that had seen better days. Once he removed the metal bit and the facets he braided two feet of the leather strands together and wrapped the remaining leather around the end to form a handle. The girls sat quietly, looking miserable as Ned methodically laced the leather together. Every now and then Amelia would look up and watch his rough hands work the strands. Bonnie gasped out loud when Ned swatted his own palm to test the effectiveness of his new implement.

Neither girl had said a word all the way back to camp after their ordeal with the outlaws. Even now in the face of imminent pain, they were too thankful for their rescue to even try to minimize their disobedience. They both rose and removed their skirts and bloomers upon Ned's command without any protest. They held hands as they both leaned into a tree and stuck out their bare bottoms. Taking careful aim, Ned brought the laced bridle down across Amelia's backside first and then on Bonnie's. The girls howled in unison as the leather striped their bare asses repeatedly.

"I'm sorry" Bonnie was the first to voice her remorse as she sobbed.

Amelia's apology wasn't far behind as the two girls took their punishment knowing it was well deserved.

When it was finally over and the girls were dressed, Ned led Bonnie to where Toby was standing on the other side of a clump of trees. Toby immediately began to comfort her as he wrapped his arms around her shaking body. Bonnie clung to him as new tears stained his shirt.

Ned returned to a forlorn Amelia and stood about three feet from her. He opened his arms invitingly. She threw herself into his chest as a wave of new sobs escaped her lips. Ned closed his eyes as he held her tight.

# THE SALOON

## Chapter 7

"See I told you we would find work," Amelia said as she pointed to the **GIRLS WANTED** sign in the window of the *Baxter Saloon*.

"I don't know," Bonnie said apprehensively. "What do we know about serving drinks?"

"What's there to know, the men tell you what they want and you give it to them," Amelia explained as she pushed through the swinging doors.

Bonnie followed her inside. Mr. Baxter, the owner, was summoned by the bartender as soon as the girls entered.

"What can I do for you?" he asked.

"We saw your sign and need a job," Amelia answered.

Bonnie looked around the room and noticed that they were getting curious looks from some of the patrons. There were several men sitting at various tables. Some were drinking, some were playing cards and one was passed out at a corner table.

"Ever worked in a saloon before?" Mr. Baxter asked.

"No but we're fast learners," Amelia answered trying to sound confident enough for both of them, meanwhile ignoring Bonnie's tug at her shirt sleeve.

"I don't think this is a good idea," Bonnie whispered to her cousin as Mr. Baxter looked over the girls from head to toe.

"Shhhh," Amelia's irritation was clearly showing. "We need to find work and here it is."

"You'll both do just fine," he said. "Go see Mrs. Semster, the dressmaker down the street, and she'll get you clothed with some new dresses. You start tonight," he said, lighting a cigar and giving his bartender a wink and a grin.

"But we don't have enough money for that," Amelia said worriedly, hoping that they didn't just lose the job before getting started.

"Don't worry. I'll take care of it. I'll deduct the cost a little each week," Mr. Baxter assured her.

"Thank you. Thank you," Amelia gushed as she urged Bonnie out the door.

***

"I don't know about this," Bonnie said as she tried in vain to pull up the bodice of her new dress. "It seems indecent."

"Don't be silly," Amelia responded with a giggle. "This is how they dress out here in the west."

"I didn't see any other women dressed like this," Bonnie grumbled to herself as she looked at her reflection in the mirror.

The girls had gotten a room to share at the boarding house when their cattle drive arrived in town the day before. They spent a few of the coins they had on a bath after the long hard trip. Ned made sure they were set up in a respectable boarding house before selling his stock.

"What do you think Mr. Crowley or Toby would say?" Bonnie asked anxiously as she plucked at the feathers on her sleeve.

"What do you mean?" Amelia asked as she turned to face her cousin. "It's none of their business what we do. Besides they should be happy we found jobs," she said.

"But I thought you and Ned were kind of sweet on each other?" Bonnie giggled.

"No more than you and that cowboy, Toby," Amelia said with a smile.

"I don't think Toby even knew I left the camp," Bonnie said sadly.

"I'm sorry Bonnie. Ned is making plans to go back to Texas. He left to sell cows without as much as a goodbye," Amelia said trying to console her.

The girls spent the next hour primping and getting ready for their first night of work.

***

"Right on time," Mr. Baxter said approvingly as he inspected his new employees. "Those dresses are just right."

"Where do we start?" Amelia asked as she glimpsed around the room and noticed several other girls similarly dressed.

"It's simple," the employer said a little embarrassed at the naivety of his new employees. "Be nice to the customers. If they want a drink, get it for them. Give them whatever they want. If they want more than a drink, the rooms are upstairs. But no one and I mean NO ONE, goes upstairs without first seeing my bartender. Got that?" he asked sternly.

Bonnie and Amelia nodded trying to hide their confusion, which was clearly written on both of their faces.

"What's upstairs?" Bonnie whispered to her cousin.

"I guess if they get tired, you know or had too much to drink like that one over there at the bar. That cowboy is about to fall out of his seat," Amelia giggled.

"HEY! Get me a whisky!" the girls heard from a table to their right.

The girls looked at each other with wide eyes.

"I'll take this one," Amelia said, patting Bonnie reassuringly on the arm. She walked over to the table with three men seated around it playing cards.

"Whisky!" a dark haired man said as he peered at Amelia over the top of his cards.

"Right away," Amelia said as she rushed over to the bar.

"You…" A middle aged man dressed in a suit pointed at Bonnie. He was sitting at the same table, his cards discarded, no longer interested in playing.

"Me?" Bonnie asked as she looked around wondering if he was actually talking to her.

"Yes, YOU!" the man said as his mustache twitched, "Come here."

Bonnie hesitated for a moment and then walked timidly toward the man with the mustache.

"Have a seat," he said as he patted his lap.

When Bonnie didn't immediately respond he grabbed her wrist and pulled her onto his lap. Bonnie shrieked with surprise as the men at the table began to laugh.

Amelia saw Bonnie's distress as she walked briskly with the dark haired man's drink. As she placed the whisky down on the table she was startled by a sudden smack to her clothed backside. Straightening sharply she moved toward her cousin.

"Let her up!" Amelia demanded as Bonnie struggled in the man's lap. The man just laughed and snaked a hand to rest possessively on Bonnie's breast.

"Please" Bonnie begged as she tried to get up.

Without warning the dark haired man grabbed Amelia around the waist and brought her down onto his knee with a resounding thud.

"Let go of me!" Amelia shouted as he began pawing at the hem of her dress, trying to reach underneath.

The men continued to laugh as the girls struggled. Feeling the man's hand on the inside of her thigh, Amelia picked up his drink and threw it into his face. He winced as the golden colored liquid burned his eyes. The shock of her actions silenced his fellow card players immediately. He stood up, bringing Amelia with him. Her look of smugness was soon replaced by outrage as he grabbed her arm and led her toward the stairs.

"Put HER on my tab!" he yelled at the bartender as he began pulling Amelia up the stairs behind him.

"I'm gonna teach you a lesson," he said through gritted teeth "and after I've blistered your ass real good, I'm gonna ride you all night till you can't walk."

Amelia struggled to pull herself free, as her fear mounted, but the man was too strong. He successfully yanked her to the top landing and as the patrons laughed and howled below, the pair disappeared down the hall to an empty room.

He shoved her into the room so hard that she tripped and landed on the floor. With his booted foot he kicked the door closed behind him. Amelia scrambled to her feet and into the corner of the room watching as he quickly released his belt buckle and pulled his belt loose from his pants.

"Time for your lesson," he said menacingly as he grabbed hold of her dress with both hands and ripped her dress completely off.

Amelia stood before him, her breasts bare with only her bloomers on. With a quick yank of his hand her bloomers were down to her ankles. He snatched them out from under her as Amelia fell forward on the bed. As her ass was sticking up into the air, the dark haired man placed a strong hand on the small of her back and with the other hand brought his belt down hard on her bare backside. Amelia yelped loudly as the leather made contact with her rounded cheeks.

***

Ned, Toby and a few other drovers entered the *Baxter Saloon* looking forward to a drink or two after the long cattle drive. Ned wanted to celebrate the good fortune of getting a great price for his cattle. He was disappointed when he went to Amelia's room to invite her out for dinner and found she wasn't there. He had something important to ask her. He wasn't surprised to find Toby knocking on their door looking for Bonnie when he arrived. When neither girl answered their knock, they decided to meet up with a few others at the saloon. The men were surprised to see Bonnie sitting in a man's lap. The dress she had on barely contained her breasts. Her nipples were barely concealed by the low cut of the cloth. Toby couldn't contain his outrage as he stomped towards Bonnie.

"Let her go!" Toby demanded as he reached down and pulled Bonnie up.

"Hey! Wait your turn I get her first!" the man protested as he got to his feet, outraged.

"Not this one!" Toby yelled as he punched the man squarely in the jaw.

The man fell to the floor and shook his head, clearly confused.

"Take her, take her," he muttered as he rubbed his sore jaw.

The bartender, having a lot of experience in defusing arguments, quickly instructed another girl to go help him up and give him something else besides a fight to occupy his interest.

Toby urged Bonnie outside. She was crying so hard it took several attempts before the men understood that Amelia was also in the saloon. Ned ran back in looking around for Amelia. When he didn't see any sign of her, he ran to the stairs. The bartender yelled for him to stop but his protests fell on deaf ears as Ned made his way up the stairs. He pushed open each door as he came to it. The first room was empty. The second door opened easily only to interrupt a cowboy as he was balling a woman on the bed. To Ned's relief the woman was not

Amelia. With his apologies he closed the door and continued down the hall until he came to the last room. He heard the cries coming from within. The door gave way easily as Ned kicked it in. Amelia was naked face down on the bed. Her bottom was crimson red. The man standing over her had just lowered his pants down to his ankles. His erection was clearly visible. Ned shoved him to the side and gave him a swift kick in the ass, causing the man to lose his balance. He fell and hit his head against the wall, knocking him out cold.

"Get UP!" he hollered at Amelia as she felt his strong arms helping her off the bed.

Ned wrapped his coat around her naked body as he led her out of the room. He put his arm around her when he saw her tear stained face. She snuggled close to him as they made their way down the stairs. Everyone in the saloon stopped to watch as the big burly rancher escorted Amelia from the bar. Ned's ranch hands followed them outside.

Seeing Amelia, Bonnie ran and put her arms around her cousin.

"Are you okay?" Bonnie asked.

Amelia could only shake her head, a little reluctant to leave Ned's side to embrace Bonnie.

"Let's get the girls out of here," Ned ordered as they all moved away from the front of the saloon.

Ned and Toby led the girls down the street to the boarding house as the other's made their way to camp.

"We'll collect their things and take them back to camp," Ned said to Toby.

The girls looked at each other without saying a word. It wasn't until their belongings were packed that Amelia spoke up.

"I'm not going!" she said flatly, ignoring the fact that she had just been saved from being raped.

"Well you ain't staying here!" Ned countered, his anger returning after hearing her defiant words.

"Yes I am," Amelia said as she put her bag on the bed. "Give me one reason why I should go with YOU!"

"Take Bonnie to camp," Ned said to Toby in a calm voice. "Amelia and I have a few things to work out."

Toby escorted Bonnie from the room. Amelia watched as her cousin meekly left with Toby, angered and feeling a little betrayed by Bonnie's complacency.

"What the devil were you thinking, taking a job at a SALOON?" Ned bellowed when the door was shut.

"Don't yell at me," Amelia said angrily as she began yanking her clothes from the bag, throwing them all round the room for effect.

"I'm gonna do a lot more than just yell at you," Ned said as he sat on the edge of the bed.

"What's that suppose to mean?" Amelia asked as she began to rub her already sore bottom.

"I'm gonna marry you!" Ned hollered as he pulled Amelia over his lap and began swatting her backside with the palm of his hand.

"You're…WHAT?" Amelia asked, stunned by his words, as he laid several sharp smacks to her behind.

"You heard me, I'm… gonna…marry…you," Ned repeated a bit slower, this time punctuating each word with a swat.

"OUCH…OUCH. What if I don't want to marry YOU?" Amelia asked haughtily as she brought her hand back to protect her sore bottom.

"You don't have a choice," he said as he stopped spanking her suddenly.

"Of course I have a choice!" Amelia yelled back still perched precariously over his knee.

"Do you really want to work in that saloon?" he asked with a heavy sigh, as he lifted her off his knee and made her stand in front of him. "If so, I'll take you back there right now and let that cowboy have at ya. Is that what you REALLY WANT?" Ned asked, beginning to lose his patience again.

"No," Amelia whispered as she hung her head.

"Pack your things," he said as he pointed to her clothes scattered all over the room.

✼✼✼

Just outside of town, Toby stopped his horse and lowered Bonnie down to the ground before dismounting.

"Why are we stopping?" Bonnie asked. "Are we waiting for Mr. Crowley and Amelia?"

"No," Toby said as he walked into the bushes, leaving Bonnie to stand by the horse.

When he emerged from the woods Bonnie saw that he had a willow switch about three feet long in his hand. He was swishing it through the air as if getting a feel for it in his hand. She backed away until she felt his horse against her back.

"What are you going to do?" Bonnie asked fearfully as he approached her.

Without answering, Toby grabbed her by the arm and led her to a nearby fallen log. Placing one foot on the log he forced Bonnie to bend over his raised knee. Her bottom turned upright, he brought the switch down on her clothed behind. After several strokes he lifted her dress. Bonnie protested when he began pulling her bloomers down.

"Please don't," she wailed as he tugged the cloth away to bare her bottom.

"No…wife…of…mine…is working in a…SALOON!" he said as he laid the switch to her cheeks over and over.

"YEEOOWW…OHHHHHHH!" Bonnie hollered with each taste of the willow branch striking across her burning buttocks.

When Toby was finished punishing Bonnie's naked flesh he threw the switch into the bushes. Bonnie lay across his knee for several minutes sobbing softly. Suddenly she stopped crying and wiped her eyes as she stood. With a look of confusion on her face she asked, "Did you say WIFE?"

"Yes, WIFE," Toby said with a grin.

Taking him completely by surprise, Bonnie reached out and threw herself into his arms. With his foot still perched on the log he lost his balance and they both fell to the ground. Bonnie winced as her bare bottom struck the hard dirt. But they were both soon laughing as Toby kissed her and began tickling her sides calling her "wife" over and over.

※※※

The evening meal was a quiet affair. Toby and Bonnie kept giving shy looks to each other. Amelia glared at Ned and only spoke when she was spoken to. Amos grumbled to himself as he rubbed his newly healed broken arm.

"Damn women, can't get rid of 'em," he mumbled as he walked around pouring coffee.

After the girls cleaned the dishes, Bonnie tried to talk to Amelia. Amelia sat dejectedly alone ignoring everyone, including her cousin. Bonnie went to sit by Toby. They whispered together for several minutes before Toby got to his feet. He helped Bonnie up and the two headed toward the woods. Ned called Toby back and the two men walked off to talk, leaving Bonnie standing alone. She could detect the sternness in Mr. Crowley's voice but couldn't make out what he was saying to Toby. She was baffled when Toby came back to her and bid her goodnight.

"Go to bed," Ned ordered Bonnie. "Toby will see you in the morning."

Bonnie turned toward the cook's wagon and slowly climbed in. She sat down with a huff and watched as Toby made up his bedroll near the fire.

Amelia sat alone on a rock staring into the fire trying to sort out all that had happened that day. She was surprised and secretly pleased with Ned's intent to marry her. However, it angered her in the same instance that he ordered her, instead of asking her, to marry him. Ned hadn't said another word to her since they left town. She was disappointed that he made no declaration of love or any feelings for that matter. She knew the exact moment when she began having feelings for him. It was when he was giving her that first spanking by the pond. His authoritativeness was what she craved. She loved his protectiveness when he declared her off limits to the rest of the men in camp. No other man was allowed to touch her, except for him. She felt safe then, but now her feelings were all mixed up. She admitted to herself how terrified she was when she was taken upstairs in the saloon. Her bottom was still bruised from the earlier beating. But she was too stubborn to even thank Ned for rescuing her. She felt miserable and didn't know what to do about it. Finally she rose and went to join Bonnie, who was now sound asleep in the wagon.

***

The next morning the cook got the girls up earlier than usual.

"Fetch firewood," he ordered as he began clanking the pots together, looking for the coffee pot.

The girls sleepily climbed down from the wagon and headed into the woods. Bonnie looked anxiously toward her cousin but Amelia ignored her and walked in the opposite direction pretending to gather branches. By the time breakfast was ready most of the cow hands had returned to camp from their night of carousing. Amelia noted everyone was there except for Ned and Toby. She hadn't seen the trail boss all morning. Maybe he changed his mind, she thought gloomily.

"Watch it!" Bonnie said angrily as she shoved Amelia away from the dish water pan.

The dirty water splashed onto Amelia. Bonnie giggled as the water seeped down the front of her cousin's dress.

"Watch it yourself!" Amelia said as she tipped the pan, dumping its entire contents on Bonnie.

"It's all YOUR fault!" Bonnie shouted, trying to hold back the tears that threatened to run down her face.

"My fault? For what?" Amelia questioned hotly.

"For getting us those lousy jobs at that saloon… for getting me into trouble," she replied, "Did you know Toby tanned my hide on our way back here?" Bonnie asked.

"You didn't have to take the job or the tanning," Amelia shouted.

Bonnie started crying and yelling back at Amelia. Soon both girls were pushing and shoving each other. No one could understand a word they were saying. Amos sat back and smiled as he watched the girls pull each other's hair. By the time Toby and Ned rode into camp, the girls were wrestling on the ground, neither one a clear winner. The men quickly pulled the girls apart.

"What's this all about?" Ned demanded of Amelia as he yanked her to her feet.

"She started it," Amelia said pointing at Bonnie.

"I did NOT!" Bonnie said defensively as Toby held her by the waist, keeping Bonnie from lunging toward her cousin.

"Are these the brides?" the man with the white collar behind them cleared his throat and asked.

The girls stared at the minister for a moment. Then they looked at each other. Their eyes took in their disheveled clothes.

"Brides?" they both asked in unison.

"That's right girls, today is your wedding day," the minister said shaking his head, trying not to laugh at the scene before him.

"You have ten minutes to get cleaned up and presentable," Ned declared as he walked the minister toward a waiting cup of coffee.

The girls rushed to change clothes, giggling the whole time, forgetting about their earlier squabble.

"I'm sorry," Amelia finally said as they were about to walk toward their waiting grooms.

"That's okay, it wasn't entirely your fault," Bonnie admitted as she affectionately hugged her cousin.

"Come on, come on and get your fannies over here!" Toby shouted impatiently.

***

"I now pronounce you man and wife," the minister said as the two pair kissed.

The cowboys whistled and hollered as Toby gave Bonnie a long and lustful kiss. In comparison and to her chagrin, Ned gave Amelia a quick peck on the lips.

After congratulations were given all around, Toby took Bonnie by the hand and led her to a secluded spot he had found earlier that morning. There he taught her the true meaning of being his wife. He slowly undressed her and marveled at her pert breasts and the blonde triangle of hair at the juncture of her legs. Bonnie quivered as he explored her body with his hands and mouth. Bonnie timidly ran her hands over Toby's body. She stepped back shyly as her fingers accidently brushed against his crotch. His erection pressed against his pants. When he couldn't stand it any longer he quickly undressed and laid Bonnie down on a blanket he had spread on the ground. She instinctively spread her legs. He entered her swiftly as she yelped at the sudden pain.

"It won't hurt again," he promised as he began thrusting.

Slowly the pain subsided and she began moving with him. She felt the unusual heaviness and mounting pressure in her loins. Toby reached down with one hand and rubbed at her clit. Bonnie moaned as she climaxed, her juices running down his cock. Toby couldn't contain his need any longer and with a final thrust he filled her with his seed.

On the other side of the camp, Ned busied himself as he looked over a map trying to decide the best route home. Amelia sat brooding by the fire. All of the ranch hands had gone back into town for one last night before they headed home. Amos went into town to load up on supplies and taste his fair share of the women at the saloon he'd heard so much about the night before. Ned and Amelia looked up when they saw a man approach on horseback. Amelia gasped when she recognized Mr. Baxter as he dismounted his horse.

"What can I do for ya?" Ned asked.

"There's a small matter of this bill," Mr. Baxter said as he handed a piece of paper to Ned.

"What's this?" Ned asked as he studied the bill.

"Well there's the cost of the two dresses and the damage to my door," Baxter explained pointing to the figures on the paper.

"Damn it," Ned muttered as he pulled his wallet out and gave Baxter a few bills.

Baxter thanked him, quickly mounted his horse and disappeared down the road.

Ned glared hard at Amelia as if trying to decide what to do. Just as Ned was about to speak Toby and Bonnie emerged from the woods. Bonnie turned red from embarrassment as Toby pinched her backside lovingly. It was clear to them that Ned and Amelia weren't getting along as well as they were. Bonnie looked uneasily at her cousin and then at Ned. The tension between the two was clearly evident. Toby announced that he and his new bride would be eating supper in town. But before they left, he walked into the brush and cut off a willow branch and handed it to Ned.

"Consider it my wedding present," Toby said as he mounted his horse with Bonnie behind him and they trotted away.

Ned sat down across the fire from Amelia. She refused to look at him and stared down at the dirt. Not sure how to start, Ned pulled the bill out of his pocket and looked at it for a long time.

"We need to talk about this bill," he finally said.

Amelia sighed heavily and continued to stare at the ground.

"Look at me!" Ned ordered.

Amelia pretended not to hear and abruptly got up and walked toward the cook's wagon. Ned jumped up and spun her around to face him.

"I'll not be ignored!" he roared impatiently.

"What do you want me to do?" Amelia asked. "I don't have any money to pay you. How do you expect me to satisfy this debt? You can take it out on my hide if you want!" she screamed uncontrollably as all her pent up emotions for the past two days burst forth.

"That's a fine idea," he said stepping closer to her.

"I didn't mean that," she quickly said coming to her senses, with the realization of what she had let herself in for. She shivered when she saw him holding the switch in his hand.

"I think you did. Deep down you know this is

what you want and deserve," he said evenly. "Now take off your clothes!" he commanded.

Amelia didn't dare defy him. She knew he was right. She had been heading for this for the last two days. She feared his punishments but they made her feel loved, even if Ned didn't use the words.

She obediently stepped out of her dress and took off her under garments. She stood before him completely nude and submissive. Ned became turned on by the sight of his new bride. He quelled his compulsion to take her right then and there, focusing on what she needed and had subconsciously been asking for.

"Turn around and grab the wagon wheel," he said sternly.

Without a word of protest Amelia faced the wagon and bent forward grabbing the wheel tightly, presenting her round backside for Ned's chastisement. He wasted no time in drawing the switch back and bringing it down across both cheeks.

"OOOHHH!" Amelia wailed as a red line appeared on her bare backside.

Silently he striped her rear until it was covered in red welts. Amelia danced around as it became difficult to stand still with each stroke to her burning ass cheeks. She began to plead for him to stop when he began switching the sensitive part of her thighs.

"Please stooop!" Amelia begged. "I'm sorrry. I'll learn to accept it," she wailed.

Ned, caught off guard by her statement, stopped suddenly.

"Accept what?" he asked perplexed.

"That you don't..." she sobbed letting the tears fall freely.

"Accept what?" Ned asked again, clearly puzzled.

"That you don't ...love me," she finished, crying harder still.

"Love ya? Of course I love ya," he said as he resumed switching her bare flesh. "I wouldn't punish ya if I didn't love ya," he added with the final stroke of the willow branch.

She laid her head down on the wagon wheel and continued to sob. Ned stood behind her and began rubbing her back.

"Would I break down a door to rescue ya if I didn't love ya?" he asked quietly.

Amelia's sobs began to subside as she listened to his words.

"I love ya and I want to protect ya," Ned continued on, finding it hard to express himself.

"I'm a rancher and I don't like flowery speeches but my feelings for ya are real enough," he finally said.

Amelia turned toward him and put her arms around his waist, nestling close to his chest. Her nakedness became more apparent to him as he stood holding her. He began kissing her long and slowly. She responded by removing his shirt and then his trousers. Soon he was naked and she stared at his erection, timidly touching it with her fingertips. He inhaled sharply. She liked the feel of him in her hand. He caressed her body as she explored his. When she took a firm hold of his cock he growled in her ear. She giggled as his breath tickled her skin. He swung her around and bent her forward, instructing her to grab the wagon wheel again. For an instant Amelia was confused and thought she was to be punished again. She began to relax as he slid his hand down her back and gently rubbed her sore backside. She gasped when he slid his hand between her legs and felt her wetness. He ordered her to spread her legs as he eased himself inside her. She cried out when she felt the pain from the fullness of him. He slowly moved in and out until he was sure she had become accustomed to his size. He reached around and began rubbing her breasts. A moan escaped her lips. He moved his hand lower and cupped her mound, his finger playing with her clit. He could feel her pussy pulse as she moaned with pleasure. She came just as he pulled his cock from her and shot his cum on her bare ass.

### ✶✶✶

At dusk, Amos rode into camp. He saw Mr. Crowley and his new bride curled up in the chuck wagon. He quietly unloaded the supplies from the pack mule and grumbling to himself about needing a new wagon as he headed back to town.

**THE END**

**Look for these other titles from C. C. Barrett:**

*BARE TO DISCIPLINE VOL. 1: M/F Spanking Erotica Discipline Stories, The Apartment Collection Vol.1*

*BARE TO DISCIPLINE VOL. 2: M/F Spanking Erotica Discipline Stories, The Apartment Collection Vol.2*

*BRANDED (Revised Edition): An Old West Spanking Tale*

*EXECUTIVE PUNISHMENT*

*PRISONER OF DISCIPLINE*

*HALFWAY HOUSE: DISCIPLINED*

*RAZOR STRAP LEGACY*

*A SPANKING RICH GOLD RUSH*

*THE SPANKING ORDER*

*STRAPS AND STILETTOS*

*PADDLING AND POLYGAMY*

*BARE TO DISCIPLINE VOL. 3: M/F Spanking Erotica Discipline Stories, Vol.3*

*THE SEA FLOGGER*

# Lines and Wrinkles

# Lines and Wrinkles

**Copyright © Stephanie Gaunt 2019**

**All Rights Reserved**

No part of this book may be reproduced in any form, by photocopying or by any electronic or mechanical means, including information storage or retrieval systems, without permission in writing from the copyright owner of this book.

ISBN 9781910693704

First Published 2019 by Print2demand

Printed and bound in Great Britain by
www. Print2demand.co.uk
Westoning

# For Nick

I'd like to thank everyone who has helped me with my poems and with the production of this book, including the Hastings Stanza Group who have been massively supportive, Brian Lawes, Danny Mooney and, of course, Nick Dent.

# Support for charities

Profits from the sale of this book will be donated to the following charities:

**The Sara Lee Trust**

This locally-based charity provides a range of services for people with cancer. I have not used these services myself in my own periods of illness, but people close to me have benefited greatly.

**Queen Alexandra College, Birmingham**

This is a special college addressing the needs of young people with autism. My grand-daughter Eve is currently a student there.

**RDA, Fairlight Hall (Riding for the Disabled Association).**

I have known of RDA since my own pony-mad days, and Eve enjoys riding at the RDA centre at Fairlight Hall when she comes to stay with us.

# My life and my poetry

**My life so far**
It is hard to believe that I am 70!
Born in Dublin, I moved to England when I was seven. My mother bred and showed dogs, and complaints about noise and my father's chaotic business endeavours meant multiple house moves around the country. With just one sister, twelve years older than me, I was a solitary, imaginative child, sent to boarding school, which I hated.

Emerging from the education system with qualifications in personnel management and business studies, I initially worked in London. I met my first husband there, and we relocated to Gloucestershire, where my daughter was born. I became a counsellor with the then National Marriage Guidance Council.

We moved to Birmingham in 1979, where I did an MSc in psychology and worked for a drug and alcohol agency. After several years as a single parent I met, and married, my second husband Nick, an academic, and acquired two step-children. I ran a social housing training and consultancy company before finishing my career working with a community housing association.

In addition, I realised a long-held ambition to own a vintage clothes shop, 'Retro Bizarre', in Moseley.

By 2011 we had both retired, the children had long gone and we moved to Hastings. My daughter, my grand-daughter and many good friends remain in Birmingham.

On arrival in Hastings I joined the Women's Institute as a way of getting to know people, and am now President of my local group and an East Sussex Federation Trustee.

Nick and I both love life in Hastings. We enjoy exploring this area and further afield, and also enjoy our holidays, particularly in Turkey.

On a more personal level, I have had three brushes with cancer, all fortunately caught early, but involving major operations. This has only enhanced my appetite for making the most of life.

**My poetry**

From childhood, I tried to write novels, but never got past the first few chapters.

On arrival in Hastings I started my Hastings Battleaxe blog, and joined the Hastings Writers' Group. My first poem was written in 2012, as an entry to an HWG competition.

The emotional and intellectual challenge of writing poetry appealed to me, as well as the practical satisfaction of being able to finish a piece of work. I joined the Hastings Stanza group when it formed in 2014, and have not stopped writing poems since.

Many of my poems have a strong narrative thread. They are all, I hope, accessible and readable. Some are light-hearted and funny, some have a more serious twist, and many have a 'sting in the tail'.

In the Memories section, many of the poems recall early childhood. It is strange that as we age, early memories seem more vivid…

Another section of poems is about Hastings and our life here, and another smaller section concentrates on travel.

Although I have categorised some poems as Random, sometimes because they experiment with form and shape on the page, the majority of these do somehow link back to my own story.

I hope you enjoy reading the poems!

# About Danny Mooney

Although Danny Mooney has prosopagnosia, (facial blindness), he spends a lot of his time drawing and painting people.

*'Making images of people helps me remember them. Making images that other people can recognise increases the level of interest and difficulty'*

He recognises people by how they move.

*'I can only make a recognisable image of someone if I see them in motion'*

Mooney sees his work as wall mounted sculpture, with paint as the medium. The physicality and texture of the paint is key. Over the years, he has made abstract and representational images on and with all manner of materials.

For the last 5 years has made painting every day on his iPad. These are always from life, and usually of the sea.

*'I love technology, and painting on the iPad is like having my sketch book and all my colours with me all the time. I live by the sea, so my choice of subject is a no-brainer'*

Danny Mooney studied at Goldsmiths and London Guildhall University in London.

He likes to combine work with travel. In the last 3 years he has had Artist in Residence posts in Barbados, Bulgaria, France and in the virtual world of podcasting.

Mooney's work has been exhibited in the UK and America, and is represented in collections in the U.K., America, Switzerland, Japan and China.

# Acknowledgments and accolades

**Harvest Time (Page 2)** was published in the Binstead Arts Poetry Competition Anthology 2017.

**Just a Baby (Page 5)** was shortlisted for the LinkAge Southwark Poetry Competition 2018, held in memory of Dame Tessa Jowell.

**A winter's night on the West Hill (Page 20)** was published in the Hastings Writers' Group Anthology, 'Strandline' 2012.

**What my WI means to me (Page 24)** won the National Federation of Women's Institutes Lady Denman Cup competition in 2014. The cup was presented to me by HM The Queen at the NFWI Centenary Annual Meeting at the Royal Albert Hall in June 2015. The poem appears here with the permission of the NFWI.

**Hastings Castle – we know so little (Page 31)** won the Hastings Week Poetry Competition 2018.

**Writer's block (Page 48)** won the Hastings Writer's Group poetry competition 2013.

# The poems

## 1 Memories

| | |
|---|---|
| Harvest time | 2 |
| A moment on the M40 | 4 |
| Just a baby | 5 |
| Child in the woods | 6 |
| Funny? That's one for you they said | 8 |
| The dog-breeder's daughter | 10 |
| In memory of Sue G | 11 |
| Therapy | 12 |
| Gobbledygook | 14 |
| Tattoo | 15 |
| Sunday night viewing | 16 |

## 2 Hastings

| | |
|---|---|
| A winter's night on the West Hill | 20 |
| Outsiders – leaving the Electric Palace | 22 |
| Autumn morning at home | 23 |
| What my WI means to me | 24 |
| Picnic in the park | 26 |
| Hung-over in Hastings | 28 |
| Sing a song of smugglers | 29 |
| A restless night | 30 |
| Hastings Castle - we know so little | 31 |

# The poems - continued

## 3 Travel

| | |
|---|---|
| Departures | 34 |
| Cornish coast path | 36 |
| It's my job | 38 |
| Phaselis, a ghazal | 40 |
| For fans of faded grandeur | 42 |
| The Birth of Venus | 44 |
| Once a Chimaera, always a chimaera | 45 |
| Return to Moseley | 46 |

## 4 Random

| | |
|---|---|
| Writer's block | 48 |
| Magic potion | 49 |
| Slugs and snails sonnet | 50 |
| Muffin-top rondeau | 51 |
| Abstract space and the dental hygienist | 52 |
| The thoughts of Kumbuka the gorilla | 54 |
| Thinking about smells… | 56 |
| It's a frog's life | 57 |
| Acanthus | 59 |
| Bed companions | 60 |
| Dot | 61 |

# 1
# Memories

# Harvest Time

I'm running to the gate
in the last light of endless summer,
pulled by the distant grumbling roar of
combine harvester, heading homewards to the farm.

How old am I? Eleven? Twelve?
Still unformed, sexless in Aertex shirt,
scabbed knees in khaki shorts.
Time ran freely then, spooling past in random snippets
of building dens, Champion the Wonder Horse, Tizer,
dead rabbits in the woods, and, at harvest time,
the huge red combine, edging down the lane.
Spiky rollers whip brambles from the verge,
long-necked chutes like dinosaur heads
graze the overhanging trees.
Hot engine breath sears my legs,
the ground trembles.

There's Charles, the farmer's son. He's old enough
to drive the thing, yet still a shouty, mocking boy.
I don't like him, but this time, as he waves,
mouthing insults I can't hear,
I see him.
I see the little hairs on his forearms
shining gold in the setting sun.

I can't wave back
my mouth's gone dry.
He shifts the machine into a different gear.
I hope he'll turn, look at me again.
He doesn't.

Indoors, they're at the table,
dogs round their feet.
I take my napkin from its ring.
'Who was driving?'
'Charles' I reply, blushing.

# A moment on the M40

It scours through the hill where trees once grew,
roaring in its chalky canyon. Swept downwards
in the metal tide, for a moment I'm a little girl again

perched on a fat brown pony.
Nose to tail, we're plodding down the woodland track.
Hooves scuff leaf-mould, saddles creak, ponies blow and snort.
Looking down, I smooth out Dandy's mane,
pat it into place. His skin quivers as I stroke his neck.
Looking up, it's like I'm flying up the beech tree columns
to touch the leafy fan-vault roof.
My happiness hurts, an actual ache inside my ribs.
*Hey! You on Dandy! Wake up and ride your pony!*
Sensing inattention, he's seized his chance,
veered off the path, grabbed a tempting tuft of grass.
I haul at the reins, heels drumming barrel flanks.
Dandy takes no notice.
Savouring his snack, chumbling and clanking on his bit,
he sighs, farts, takes his time,
then ambles back to join the line.

Could the track have crossed just there?
Too late, we're speeding past the place.
Chalk cliffs fall away, revealing sunlit plain.
I look ahead, eyes on the wide horizon,
yet inside, I feel that childhood ache again.

# Just a baby

Like autumn leaves, memories drift
down winding pathways, heap in corners.
Raking through the past,
I pick a random fragment,
tattered, yellowed, full of holes.
I was just a baby.
                                    Shiny
                              brown button
                      shoes and white socks.
               First one foot, then the other.
               Shoes are stiff. Dad has my hand.
               Where's my sister?  There she is,
               lying face-down in the long grass,
                  not moving. There's the pony
                  with reins dangling, grazing.
                  Dad runs to her. I sit down
                  on nappy-padded bottom.
                    She looks up. Blood all
                      around  her  face,
                        down her front.
                          She's crying,
                            so am
                               I

Autumn has turned to winter.
Only her and me left now.
'That's nonsense,' she snaps.
'You weren't even there.
You were just a baby.'

# Child in the woods

You heard it.
A faint droning hum beyond those trees.
You pushed through chest-high bracken
batting at clouds of new-hatched flies
buzzing chain-saw loud.
Why did you leave the path?


You smelt it.
A sickly sweet
throat-catching stench.
You swallowed, held your nose.
Half knowing yet compelled to look,
Why did you carry on?


You saw it.
A grey furry skin
flattened on the ground.
Not living but alive,
seething with maggots.
Why was that not enough?


You got a stick.
Poked its sad white tail scut,
prodded empty eyes until
the rotted muzzle fell apart.
Then you ran away.

One day you may forget your name,
lose your loved ones' faces, but
that wormy rabbit grin will never leave you.

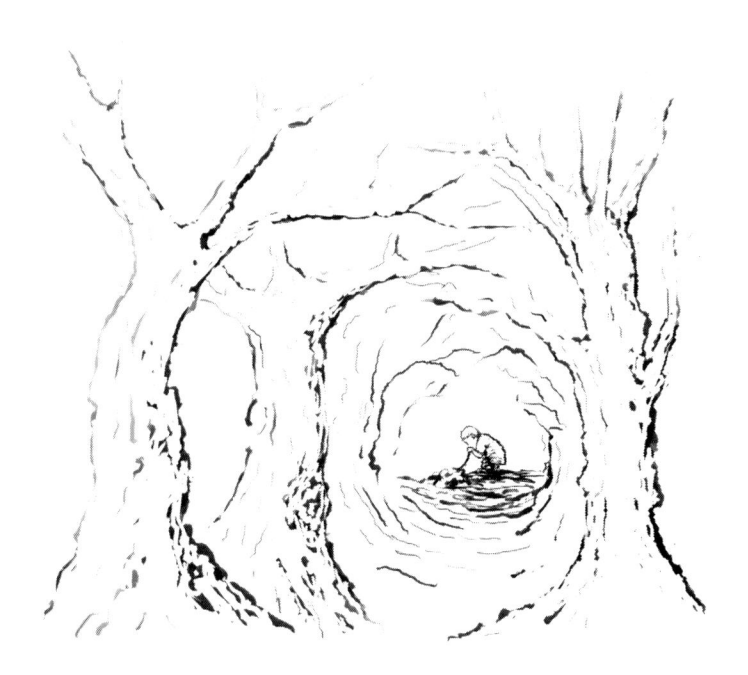

# Funny? That's one for you, they said…

*Our poetry group was given a task to write a humorous poem. My colleagues turned to me…*

I learned that lesson young…

> *My mother had a boyfriend,*
> *His name was Ambrose Spong.*

The prefects lounge
damp-haired and bored
beside the hissing gas fire.
I'm standing on a chair.
Dry mouthed with fear
I stammer out the lines I've learned,
probably a Shakespeare sonnet.
Medusa-like, they stare and sneer,
comb their snaky hair.
'You contribute nothing to the House.'
'You're such a boring little thing…'

> *My mother had a boyfriend,*
> *His name was Ambrose Spong.*
> *Did he wear a toupee?*

Now, I'm laughing with the gang.
We're throwing dirty water, soaking Fatty's bed.
Her baggy knickers billow from the fire escape.
'Look at the cry-baby!'
'Can't she take a joke?'
Those knicker flags were my idea.
So funny.
Look at me, I'm fitting in. I've found my place.

> *My mother had a boyfriend,*
> *His name was Ambrose Spong.*
> *Did he wear a toupee?*
> *No, I've got that wrong!*

Looking back, of course I feel ashamed.
But funny? Oh yes, that's still one for me…

> *The boyfriend with the toupee was staying for the night*
> *I tried to watch him take it off,*
> *Instead I got a fright.*
> *I'd hid outside his bedroom door,*
> *peering at a crack…*
> *he'd dropped his pants and trousers,*
> *but at least he'd turned his back!*

# The dog-breeder's daughter

What's that on the towel?
A new-born puppy, silent, lifeless.
*Why aren't you in bed?* That's my mother,
bent over a box in the corner. She doesn't look at me.
In the box, her prized champion bitch groans and strains,
scrabbling at blood-stained newspaper.
Seeing me, the dog quietens, briefly slaps her tail.
*Stop distracting her, there's another on the way.*

I wrap the discarded puppy in the towel,
rub it, shake it upside down.
*Leave that, it's dead.*
My shaking gets more violent.
Prising open the jaws, I blow into its mouth,
warm the limp body inside my pyjamas.
There's a kick against my chest.
Sides heaving, flailing blindly,
the puppy bubbles from its nostrils,
bats its head against my hand.

I put the squealing puppy in the box.
The bitch eyes it for a moment,
licks it roughly, rolls it over,
pushes it towards a teat.

*Well done,* says my mother, straightening up.
*It's a miracle, you've given it life.*
I'm happier with her words of praise.

# In memory of Sue G

I shiver in the shallows of the hotel pool
as she knifes through the water, up and down.
Her bow wave smacks the sides, sucks into corners,
slaps the pasty chests of businessmen
lounging by the rail. Idly, they eye the angles
of her wiry frame, catch each other's eyes,
smirking, dismissive. I look away.

She powers to the wall, kicks, turns and dives.
We're here for the money, paid well by men like
these to do their dirty work, justify their lies.
She surfaces beside me, beckoning and brisk.
Feebly, I flounder in her wake.

Our clients talk of managed change, refocused
business aims. We have to talk of loss.
Lost jobs, lost hopes, lives turned upside down.
Those rows of anxious faces. When shock turns to rage
I haver and dissemble, afraid to meet their eyes,
then call for Sue. Courageous, positive, she stares
them down, slicing through their fear and pain.

Then Sue gets ill.
'Battling cancer to survive,'
'Positive thinking wins the day,'
Don't believe a word of it.
Sue's strong, she fights, for a while
she swims against the tide.
But in the end she falters, drifts away,
while I, the coward, stay alive.

# Therapy

The counsellor tugs the neckline of her jumper,
fingers touching skin for reassurance. It's late,
she's tired. At last the client begins to talk.
*He gets that wound up in that fuckin' flat, it's true.*
*Babby's screaming, he's got no job, what's a man to do?*

The counsellor smells the woman's sweat,
her rain-soaked steamy coat. Where's that
air freshener? On the table by the tissue box…
*They've strapped me ribs, they know me now at A and E.*
*I tripped. Fell headlong down the stairs, you see.*

The counsellor sees the clock hands move.
She's getting nowhere. Her case notes
will be blank, no results to show.
*I'm that half-soaked! He says I'm just a clumsy cow,*
*always falling over things, don't ask me how!*

The counsellor gets impatient, goes too far.
'You tell me that you tripped and fell.
I think he hit you, pushed you. Am I right?'
*You're the expert love, so you must know best…*
*If you were me, what would you do next?*

So easy, thinks the counsellor…

> Pack a bag, take the child and go.
> Or wait until he sleeps,
> and bash him with a pan
> not hard enough to kill,
> just to show you can.
> Get a hammer, just for fun
> smash his fingers one by one.
> Before he wakens from his 'nap'
> pour boiling water in his lap…

The counsellor tastes blood,
she bit her tongue too hard.
'I'm here to listen, not to give advice.
Our hour is nearly up. How time flies…

Same time next week?'

# Gobbledygook

*'Jim? Where are you? Are you ever going to draw that bird?'*
My father dumps the turkey on the table.
He shrugs off his jacket, knots an apron
round his belly, sighing blasts of whisky breath.
Wicker baskets creak, dogs seethe round his legs
as he sharpens the knives.

Bam. Off with its head.
Bam Bam. I grab the severed feet,
pull sinews, clench the scaly toes.
'Look at me! I'm a bird monster!'
My bloodied fists sprout Harpy claws
as I run to scare my mother.

He throws red gobbets to the dogs,
opens up the gizzard, scrapes out
turkey's final meal. I pick tiny shining
pebbles from the yellow shredded grass.
'Look carefully, you may find diamonds,'
says my father.

Years pass, so many turkeys, all gobbled up.
Do I see the ghostly flock file past me
across a bright celestial meadow?
They browse on fragrant herbs,
peck at sparkling dewdrops
glinting in the sun.

# Tattoo

Needles buzz, a wasp swarm shrill above the pounding bass.
Noise rattles the colour bottles, red, yellow, black and blue.
Across the room, a man moans, thrashing feebly
like a beetle on its back. His watching woman shrieks,
dragons on her massive arms shudder as she laughs.

I'm lying quietly, studying the ceiling cracks.
A boy pulls up a stool beside me. He's skinny,
dressed in black, hands etched with Celtic runes.
He surveys my stomach. To me, the scar's a loudmouth,
shouting threats and accusations.
To him, it's a canvas, just another job.
He mixes colours, snaps on latex gloves, pulls a lamp across.
I hear the needle's angry whine.
Cutting the pattern line is hard. He holds his breath,
flexes his fingers. He needs a steady hand.
I picture the pain as scarlet cloth, wiping out the past,
but the boy keeps on talking. The cloth floats away.
Now, a different pitch of buzz, a prickling, stinging pain.
Colour needles, shading in my cobra's tail.

At last it's done. He holds a mirror, we both inspect.
The ugly weal has vanished. Cancer's evil rant is silenced,
muffled in the serpent's coils. It's magic.
*'You'll be wearing your bikini now!'*
The magician laughs, unwraps a piece of gum.

# Sunday night viewing

The sea glows sunset pink. I draw the curtains, glimpse
                the neighbour's telly.
A tiny Poldark, shirtless, emerges from the waves.
                I flop onto the sofa
doing that older person's grunty sigh. The cat yawns and
                stretches,
husband wakes. 'Just resting my eyes.' Poldark buttons up
                his breeches.
The latest episode in my Sunday evening serial life.


Was there once another Poldark? A different husband,
                sofa fresh from Habitat?
70's shag pile carpet, empty Cotswold darkness beyond
                the patio door.
A fractious baby on my knee, arching her back, banging
                her hot damp head against
my aching breast. I'm exhausted. The memory blurs.
                Perhaps it wasn't even Poldark.
Tall ships and tricorn hats… Was it the Onedin Line?

Bergerac drives across the screen. Must be 1980s.
      No husband now, yet someone's
on the sofa. He's faceless, just passing through. Harsh
      city street lamps show up
toy-strewn floor, felt-tip on the wall. Cat's meowing,
      I forgot its food.
Another week tomorrow, school clothes, work clothes,
      dinner money.
I watch the pictures flicker on the screen but know I've
      lost the plot.


Mr Darcy's swimming with his clothes on. It's 1995.
      I'm multitasking
with a glass of wine, tomorrow's meeting notes beside me
      on the sofa.
Cat purrs by the fire, long William Morris curtains frame
      twilight trees outside.
Cleaning lady comes on Monday, I'll tidy up. Children?
      Not quite left home…
Husband's shouting: 'I can't hear the telly! Turn that
      frightful racket down.'

Years have passed. I can't miss Downton Abbey, though
the telly's
balanced on a packing case. Our new house is curtainless,
sofa's still in store.
We said goodbye to Birmingham, left friends and family,
gave the cat away.
Husband clatters in the half-done kitchen, pops a cork,
emerges with a tray.
'Here's to Hastings and our new life by the sea!'

# 2
# Hastings

# A winter's night on the West Hill

*This is the first poem I ever wrote, submitted for a Hastings Writers' Group competition in 2012. It is based on a true story, a murder that took place some years ago in the little house we rented when we first came to Hastings.*

The winter sea draws an iron-grey line below
billowed clouds of snow. Puffer-swaddled
shoppers trudge homewards up the steps,
breath steaming in the street-light glow.

Tucked tidy in their curving row,
the waiting houses hug the hillside.
A gull stands guard on every chimney,
fierce-eyed, fluffed against the cold.

Fishing families lived here once, I'm told.
Big red-armed women scrubbed at spuds
while skinny kids picked scabby knees.
Salt-stained sea-boots waited by the door

Now, here's my friendly next-door
neighbour, come to share a cup of tea.
'It's peaceful here, despite what happened.
Oh… So sorry dear, I thought you knew…'

Alone again, I stare around me,
Hear the bumping on the stairs
As he dragged her down and killed her,
right here, where our sofa stands.

She didn't scream, the neighbour said,
she didn't want to wake their child.
'It's over now,' he'd said at last,
then the house was still once more.

He'd wrapped her body in a duvet,
hid her in the attic space.
Six days she lay there undiscovered,
right there, just above our bed.

I whisper 'Are you up there?' Silence,
then from above, I hear the gull's faint call.
So many joys and sorrows, births and deaths,
this old house has seen them all.

# Outsiders: leaving the Electric Palace

Credits roll, the lights go up.
We struggle with our coats, edge
round the roaring voices, wave at
half-known faces in the downward press.
'Who's that woman?' 'No idea, she was in
the Lilac Room, trying on a dress'.

On the rain-washed High Street
mist clouds the street lamps. Railings are
transformed, strung with droplet pearls.
We peer into shops, admire a painting of a hare,
two rusty urns, a yellow vintage bag,
a mid-century modern chair.

Quick glances into cottage windows
play a flick-book of other, settled lives.
We don't like to stare. A bar door opens,
like moths, we're attracted by the light.
There's laughter, a beery waft of warmth.
'Too crowded. Not for us tonight.'

Turning down the narrow twitten
our footsteps echo off the brick, then stop.
A fox is standing at the end. Cold yellow eyes
assess us. Outsiders. He flicks his brush, then turns.
Unimpressed, this proper Old Town resident
trots away towards the Bourne.

# Autumn morning at home

Last night the badgers came. Ravaged the lawn.
He's out in the garden, hunched against the wind,
dressing-gown flapping round his bony knees,
stamping on muddy tussocks,
kicking dew-soaked yellow leaves.
Those slippers will be ruined.

Standing by the window, I spoon up muesli.
Radiators, wakened by the chill, clank and tick.
Outside, the sun has pressed the snooze button.
It's duvet-wrapped in mist,
cradled in wind-rocked trees.
The cat meows for food.

A dark line bisects my view. Cloud-swept sky above,
leaden sea below. White flecks strew the grey.
It looks rough out there.
All at once the sun's awake,
flings a silver wash across the waves. I'm dazzled.
The toast pops up.

# What my WI means to me

*This poem won the National Women's Institute Lady Denman Cup in 2014. The cup was presented to me by the Queen at the NFWI Centenary Annual Meeting at the Royal Albert Hall in June 2015.*

I see the women walking on the beach,
talk and laughter snatched by the breeze, dipped by the waves,
feet scrunching on the shingle.
Young women, old women, all shapes and sizes.
I'm there too. I belong.

A clump of sea-kale catches our attention,
we sniff foam-white flowers above dark crinkled leaves.
'Can you eat it?' 'Yes, indeed,
pick when it's young and tender, steam like spinach.'
I listen. It's always good to learn.

Gathering shells and wave-smoothed twigs,
we share ideas. 'Let's make wreaths, or hanging mobiles,
sell them at the next bazaar.'
Thinking, I hold a piece of sea-glass to the sun.
I join in. Making things is fun.

The shifting pebbles bank up high, too steep.
Hands reach out to help each woman make the climb.
Scrambling, we arrive together,
laughing, shaking stones from sandals, panting, holding sides.
I help. I am helped in turn.

Now we wander inland along the rutted track,
the village is ahead, we can almost see the café sign.
'I'd really love a cup of tea.'
'A scone for me, and the fruit-cake's really good, they say.'
I like cake. I'll enjoy a piece today.

# Picnic in the park

We met at the bandstand. What were we like!
Down in the park, on a damp summer night

with bags and bottles, a crusty pork-pie,
not forgetting the cake – we're the WI…

'I just felt rain', 'There's a drop on the path,'
'Pork pie will go soggy.' We just had to laugh.

Anxious now, we peered up at the sky,
clouds looking heavy, not wet, but not dry.

We hurried across to a large copper beech,
and sheltered quite happily underneath.

Unfolded our chairs and shook out the rugs,
got out the glasses, unpacked the mugs.

We opened the wine and passed it around.
'Tastes just like paint-stripper!' 'Only three pounds!'

We ate chicken legs, quiche, and of course cake,
told stories, got stuck in a heated debate.

Someone fell off her stool and squashed the pork pie,
we laughed so hard we thought we would die.

Some blokes jogged right by us, we cackled like witches,
they flexed their muscles, we were in stitches.

'Look! Boot Camp Fitness!' 'Oh what a farce!'
But then, to loud music, on a flat patch of grass

they took off their tops and star-jumped around,
until one of us snapped 'It's not their private ground!'

Next thing, she'd marched over, told them what for,
we couldn't quite hear, but it looked like she swore.

The men sort of shrivelled, then scuttled away,
our champion returned, red-faced from the fray.

We laughed even more, gave each other high fives,
before settling down quietly to talk of our lives.

A young seagull flew down, he looked so alone,
we threw him the pork pie, then we went home

# Hung-over in Hastings

*This is a palindrome or mirror poem, where the words in the second half of the poem exactly mirror those in the first half.*

Darkness
curtains drawn
too much light now
Flinching. Glitter-ball strobing sun and sparkling sea.
Ships passing, sharp faceted jet, hazed horizon.
Suddenly swooping gull shadow, screeching.
Pounded plumped pillows, lumpy, restless,
blinking. Dancing sun-beamed dust, scratchy.
Dressing-table glinting prisms, bottle rainbows,
looking-glass mirrors shimmering sea.
Squinting, I turn over.
Too bright.
Over I turn, squinting.
Sea, shimmering, mirrors looking-glass.
Rainbow bottle prisms, glinting dressing-table
Scratchy dust sun-beamed, dancing, blinking.
Restless. Lumpy pillows plumped, pounded,
screeching shadow gull swooping suddenly.
Horizon hazed, jet faceted sharp passing ships.
Sea sparkling, sun strobing glitter-ball. Flinching.
Now light too much,
drawn curtains.
Darkness.

## Sing a song of smugglers

'Hey Jack! Heft that barrel higher!'
Stick your finger in your ear.
Sing a song of jolly smugglers,
fill your tankard, quaff your beer.

Sing of ponies, hooves muffled,
trotting down a moonlit track.
Finest silk for ladies' ruffles…
Brandy Vicar? Baccy in this sack!

All join the chorus, sing along!
Watch the friendly lanterns winking
for our smugglers, brave and strong.
Let's drink to Merrie England's song!

Sing of drug mules' stuff and swallow,
choking deaths in lorry tombs,
starving children locked in basements,
trafficked women beaten blue.

All join the chorus, sing along!
Watch the rubber dinghies sinking
for our smugglers, brave and strong
Let's drink to Merrie England's song!

# A restless night

I open my eyes.
A shriek rips away the silence.
Anxious, clammy, I push away the duvet,
watch faint shadows knife across the window blind.
Gull parents dive, screaming, from the roof,
desperate to save their one remaining chick
from nameless prowling danger in the dark.
Half-awake, my bed companion flops on his back,
throws out his arms like a startled new-born.
His breathing stutters, shifts from peaceful sighs
to rasping, bubbling snores.

I kick him, carefully, just hard enough.
He snorts, grabs the bedclothes, turns,
settles back to silent sleep.
I close my eyes.
The gulls go quiet.
Light creeps round the edges of the blind,
sparrows chatter, pigeons call,
gull chick peeps for food.
The threat has passed
with the night.

# Hastings Castle – we know so little

*This poem won the Hastings Week Poetry Competition 2018. The theme was 'Views of Hastings Castle'.*

Walking on the West Hill, you can't see the Castle,
just a flattened mound between the trees.
Let's imagine William, riding back from Battle.
What's the view the weary Conqueror sees?
His castle is roughly built of wood, bounded by a
strong stockade. Wild Haestingas might invade…

Maybe sentries shout 'How went the day?'
as they unbar the gate. The exhausted army
straggles through. What might the soldiers say?
'Great victory!' 'Harold dead on Senlac Hill,'
'God Save King William!' No, none of that,
the Normans all spoke French.

We think the army marched along the Ridge.
Did they pass the wild-haired women, weeping,
running to the field to find their fallen men?
Was Edith Swan-Neck out there with the rest?
Legend says she found her Harold's naked corpse.
Did she recognise tattoos or love-bites on his chest?

What of the Haestingas? Did they help rebuild
the Castle as a fortress, in forbidding stony grey?
Our Old Town was a muddy marsh, ships anchored
in the harbour where Marks and Spencer's is today.
Haestingas town is drowned, somewhere over there…
We can share their Castle view by standing on the Pier.

We know so little of our history. A jumble
of disjointed fragments, scattered, some lost for ever
like stones falling from the Castle when it tumbled
down the cliff. Views of the gap-toothed ruin
dominate our town. Although we see it every day
it keeps its secrets firmly locked away.

# 3
# Travelling

# Departures

Once through those sliding doors,
you're a creature to be processed,
roped in a hair-pin queue for Bag Drop.
Woman tags the cases, doesn't meet your eyes.

Later, lighter, shorn of heavy baggage,
the herd heads upwards to Security.
Boarding pass on the scanner,
men in body armour watch, blank-faced
as the gate stays shut.
Paper's upside down.
Try again.

This line is moving slowly yet too fast.
No time to load the plastic tray,
knots in laces, hands shaking.
Blue-jowled man chews gum
as he bangs the tray back into line.
Rolling forward, it disappears
through flapping curtain strips.

Hesitate, a sheep arriving at the dipping trough,
then scuttle through the arch.
It bleeps.
Lights flash, you're shed from the flock,
and penned, spread-limbed, in a plastic tube,
exposed to all eyes.
Someone feels your body up and down,
looking past your shoulder.

Has the bag got through the scanner?
Where's the plastic tray?
Shunted to a siding.

Slalom through a shining maze,
the Duty Free forest of temptation.
Like serpents coiling from the branches,
women brandish hissing perfume sprays.

Corralled in the Departure Lounge.
Pause to browse and graze until
Boarding Gate is opened.

Herd stampedes down endless corridors,
belts along the travellators,
crowds into another, smaller pen.
Find a plastic chair, assess the others.
Pray you're not seated near that baby.

Speedy Boarding? Not today.
Like cows at milking time, wait for ever
by the magic door until the rope's undone.

Shuffle down a narrow passage, clatter across
the air-bridge towards a lighted door.

'Welcome Aboard.'

# Cornish Coast Path

In dreams, I float in limpid rain-washed light.
Colours glow inside my head, sunny postcard bright.
Golden gorse against blue sky, orange lichened stone,
turquoise tumbling sea, fringed with lacy foam.

I hear a skylark's trill, gull's distant mewing call,
waves murmer as they break, then softly fading, fall.
My mind's-eye path is trackless, yet meanders on ahead.
I have no feet, yet smell crushed ramsons where I tread.

Today, it's real. I trudge along the rocky path. The line
of friends ahead don't pause, they're leaving me behind.
All alike in zipped-up fleeces, day sacks, sturdy boots,
we scuff our feet on shifting scree, trip on tangled roots.

The hearty ones in front stride out, a bit too fast for me.
Violets hide beside the path, I stop and stoop to see
as leaders pull away, gaps open in the rank.
I'm catching up, flowers unseen, abandoned on the bank.

Stomping through the brambles, last year's bracken rust,
I scramble up rock steps, breath screaming in my chest.
We smile for photos, posed by a granite stack,
watch rollers fold and break, cold stone against our
                                            backs.

Colours glow before my eyes, sunny postcard bright
golden gorse against blue sky, limpid rain-washed light.
But my mind's moved on, it's in the pub, the finish of
                                                  our ramble.
It's half-past one. We've left it late. Will we get a table?

# It's my job

*This was inspired by a visit to the Yorkshire Sculpture Park. We encountered a young employee cleaning a massive Henry Moore sculpture.*

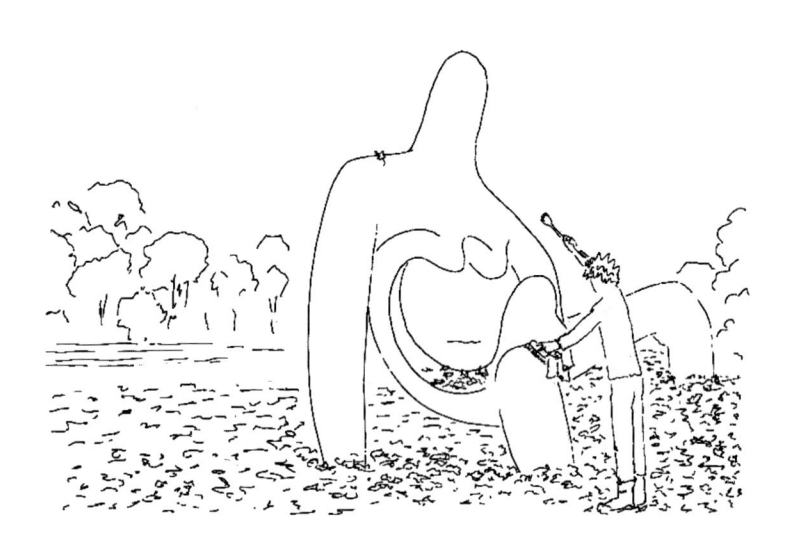

Sponge her basalt flank. Dip into bucket, steaming
in the morning chill. Clear wind-blown leaves from
buttock curve, sweep massive, elongated thigh.
She's reclining, but her head is far too high
to reach. I have to use my brush.

Her belly's hollow, stone enclosing space.
I whirl my cloth round sunlit sky, catch key-hole
glimpse of trees reflected in the lake.
Shadowed dew drops bead her polished flesh
like perspiration, caught between her breasts.

Gently now, concentrate. Swab the infant's head.
Some wretched bird has done its business.
Big white splodges here… and here, across its bum.
Careful, don't scratch the priceless stony skin.
Mum's faceless, yet I sense she's watching me.

Visitors trudge across the grass, cameras in hand.
An old man waves his stick, mutters to his friend.
I've spoilt their view. She should be solitary, ruler
of the landscape, magically shiny, mysteriously clean.
Sorry folks! I grab my things and quickly back away.

What would you prefer to see? Bird shit on the baby?
You'd soon complain. Take your snaps, pose for selfies,
hurry up and go away. I've got to wash her plinth,
then I'm on the Paolozzi after Henry Moore. That's
all fiddly lines and corners. Just another chore.

# Phaselis, a ghasal

*A ghasal (or guzzell as it should be pronounced) is an ancient Islamic verse form, favoured by early middle-Eastern and Turkish poets. It has an intricate, repeating rhyme scheme. The last couplet should always include a reference to the poet.*
*Phaselis is a ruined Graeco/Roman city in Turkey, on the Lycian coast, a few miles from Cirali, where we like to spend our holidays.*

A crisp packet blows across the agora, disappears beneath
    the over-arching pines.
Maybe, entombed below the shattered columns, a poet,
    eternally lamenting, pines

for the long-dead city. His elegy is lost, forgotten,
    smothered in a needle shroud.
Trees rule here now, breaking through the temple floor, a
    hypostyle of soaring pines.

Cones strew the triumphal way where Alexander rode,
    past gap-toothed lines
of plundered plinths, pushed aside by triffid roots of
    steadily advancing pines.

I'm settled on a marble block beside the harbour wall.
    Time blurs and shifts. Across
the blue a distant drumbeat sounds, above the hum of
    cicada-thrumming pines.

The heavy rhythm pounds inside my head. Is it driving
    banks of oars, a shackled,
straining crew? A mighty trireme, come to save the city
    from still-invading pines?

No, it's a boom-boom boat. Crew boys shout, waves
    suck and slap at ancient stones,
anchor rattles down. On deck, ranks of pink-fleshed sun-
    slaves sprawl, supine,

sound-consumed. Fleeing, I stumble, lose a flip-flop.
    Needles find my tender toes.
This lesser poet's lines are also lost, forgotten in the pain
    from stabbing spines

# For fans of faded grandeur

## *The Palacio Imperial Hotel Grand Canary*

*This Splendid Hotel, designed by an eminent English Architect and erected by a leading English Company, is now open for the accommodation of visitors for the 1884 Winter Season.*

*Patronised by Members of the Reigning Families of Europe*
*The Hotel stands in its own beautiful Gardens, beside the Sea-shore Promenade, close to the Steamer landing-stage.*

**DINING SALONS AND DRAWING ROOMS, LADIES' ROOM, READING AND WRITING ROOMS, BILLIARDS AND SMOKING ROOMS.**

*Carriages to hire and Horses for riding. Beautiful sands with capital sea bathing and boating.*
*Resident English physican. Near English Church.*
*Direct steamer communication and mails to England every three days.*

The chandeliers in the breakfast salon tinkle,
tarnished drops protesting as lorries rumble past
too near the parakeet-laden palms, the ghostly statues
hidden in the tangled garden. The motorway is in a
concrete chasm, severing hotel from sea.

A container ship edges into view, a sheer metal cliff
blotting out the sun. Harried by hooting bath-toy tugs
it creeps towards the looming cranes, its oily wake
rattling plastic bottles against the dockside wall.

Inside, the coffee machine is broken yet again.
Spanish students lounge on tipped-back chairs,
comparing selfies amid half-eaten croissants.
Their laughter echoes off frescoed nymphs
cavorting on the damp-stained ceiling.

In the corner, an English couple
mop their lips on frayed napkins,
monogrammed 'Palacio Imperial'.
They nod and smile at a passing waiter.
'Gracias', they say in careful Spanish.
He stares at them disdainfully.
Standing up, the pair are reflected in a spotted mirror.
The distorted image wavers, fades and disappears
as they leave the room.

# The Birth of Venus

*Painted by Botticelli in the 1480s, the 'Birth of Venus' hangs in the Uffizi Gallery, Florence. It is one of the most famous images in the world, said to epitomise the Western ideal of female beauty.*

> Push through the crowds to catch a glimpse,
> tick her off our list of top ten sights. Just
> a pleasant picture of a pretty young girl.
>
> Blown towards us on her scallop shell,
> eyes averted, she looks demure, innocent,
> a short-lived flower pressed flat to the canvas.
>
> One hand fails to conceal her breasts,
> the other frames her Barbie-bare pudenda
> with flowing waves of gilded hair.
>
> She's air-brushed perfect, marble pale,
> a soft-porn pin-up for a Medici banker,
> contrived for his solitary pleasure.
>
> The scallop shell floats close to shore,
> another goddess hurries with a robe.
> Too late, I've seen Venus naked.
>
> I recognise that hip-jutting model pose
> as she prepares to join our man-made
> woman's world.

## Once a Chimaera, always a chimaera

Swathed in heavy velvet Turkish dusk,
we struggle upwards, slapping mosquitos
on sweat-pooled skin, feet rubbed raw.
It's worth the pain to see those fabled flames.

The Chimaera monster once lived up here,
belching fiery death. Entombed by Bellerophon,
it's said her female power still burns, fanned
by the feathered wings of Pegasus.

In the ancient world, the flares were famous,
a fiery pharos guiding Grecian triremes,
a glowing beacon for gilded barquentines,
bound for far Byzantium.

The summit is crowded. Where are the fires
that bred the monstrous myth? We smell toasting
marshmallows, patchouli, sweat. Women dance,
breasts bouncing, holding hands, circling

feeble flickers sputtering from scattered clefts,
like flames on kitchen gas rings. Shrinking from
the noise, the flashing phones, dodging selfie sticks,
we retreat into darkness, seeking the

tumbled temple of Hephaestus. Two men
crouch behind a marble block, guarding something
half-hidden in the scrub. Could it be a gas cylinder?
Or is it a chimaera?

# Return to Moseley

My feet understand these pavements, avoiding root-snagged flagstones, stepping over slick brown drifts of leaves. Red-brick villas doze in misty bird-song gardens between the dripping trees. A startled squirrel scuttles up the nearest trunk, bounds across the road on a fragile bridge of twigs.

Back then, I thought the air was fresh. Now I catch a faint metallic city tang behind scents of damp conifer, late roses, hints of curry wafting from a lifted sash. Pans rattle, women chatter in Punjabi. It all feels comfortable, the same, yet it's different. I don't live here anymore.

The next house has changed. A new white Audi, parked beneath the copper beech on the freshly gravelled drive, potted bay trees flank an elegant front door. But I spot shredded kebab boxes under the privet hedge, my lip curls at that old familiar stench, the feral whiff of fox.

A punk band once lived across the road. I remember druggy shouting, stained net curtains, empty beer cans ranged along the sill. Today the house is empty, waiting. The gate is boarded up, a builder's sign planted in the fly-tipped bramble patch that will one day be a lawn.

Here's our old home. I dawdle past, desperate to see yet not wanting to be seen. The paintwork's fresh, the monkey-puzzle tree has gone. Through the window I glimpse a man in cord trousers making up the fire. A stranger. I walk on. It's just another Moseley house.

# 4
# Random

# Writer's block

I have to write a poem today. In fact, I have to find
up to forty rhyming lines. The deadline's near, it niggles, cold,
a wet patch on the mattress that passes for my mind.
Thoughts, like naughty children, tumble, bounce and play.
I try to pin them down, but they laugh and run away.

Let's check my emails. Junk. Delete. Home insurance due.
Shall I go ahead and pay? Or 'Go Compare', the prudent way?
No time, I have to write. Click the box that says 'Renew'.
New messages appear. Delete. This junk's a pain…
Oh look, what's this? News from old friend Sal in Spain.

She poses, white teeth and crepy tits, beside a villa pool.
Glass raised, brittle bright against the blue. Who is this
tangoed stranger? The gawky girl I knew at school?
That Spanish sun has made her skin just shrivel…
Get back to the poem. How can I write such drivel?

Too late. Slippers slopping down the hall, fridge door closes.
Ice cubes chink against a glass; a pause, and then he's calling:
'Your G and T's outside! There are greenfly on the roses…'
'I'm coming down. Hang on, I'll find the spray.'
Better save, shut down computer. No more work today.

I have to write a poem. Tomorrow I'll really have to find
up to forty rhyming lines. Deadline's near, it niggles, cold…
stop…I've said that once. Repetition undermines a poem,
or does it strengthen? Looks alright, but I don't know.
Where did I put that greenfly spray? Down the stairs I go.

# Magic potion

Sham uncles breathing beer, plucking coins from hairy ears.
'Take a card, any card!' No, don't come near me….,
'Come closer dear, what have I here?' Just go away.
Busty spangled ladies in false-bottomed boxes,
scarves spool from nostrils, doves shit with fear.
New-style witches invoke Mother Earth, brew potions
on the Aga, chant healing mantras on sweaty yoga mats.
Old-style witches wore tattered black, communed with cats,
sold herbs and spells to make unwanted babies disappear.
Black magic, white magic, dancing naked in the woods.
Boy wizards on broomsticks, Hollywood magic-lite.
Ouija boards and tilting tables
tea-leaves and tarot cards
guardian angels
crystal balls
tantric sex
holy grail
voodoo
runes
Forget all that.
Not my kind of magic.
I'll sprinkle sand-grain seeds on dampened soil and wait.

# Slugs and snails sonnet

Lacy lettuce leaves slick with silver trails.
Slugs, condom-ribbed, fleshy beige and black,
obese, replete, entwined with sleeping snails.
A pot full of pests, prised writhing from their cracks.
Captured, the slimy things crawl up the sides,
stalky eyes unfurling, they're headed for the rim.
Pale bellies ripple, determinedly they glide,
feelers touch my hand, quickly shrink back in.
What happens now? Of course they have to die.
Squash them? Much too messy. Sprinkle with salt
and see them fizz, as tortured bodies liquefy?
No. They're desperate to live. It's not their fault.
Lurking out of view, where the shrubs grow tall,
I throw the pesky gastropods over next-door's wall.

# Muffin-top rondeau

*A Rondeau is a French verse form, fifteen lines long, consisting of three stanzas: a quintet, a quatrain, and a sestet with a rhyme scheme as follows: aabba aabR aabbaR. Lines 9 and 15 are short - a refrain (R) consisting of a phrase taken from line one.*

No muffin top. Roll of fat replaced
with proper curvy nipped-in waist.
I won't eat cake, or sweets or chips,
fattening food won't pass my lips.
This chocolate? What an awful waste

to throw it out, there's no real haste,
just one more square… another taste…
'Moment in the mouth, lifetime on the hips.'
No muffin top.

The sad reality must be faced,
my wobby bits will never be erased.
I'll wear bigger jeans. It's no disgrace.
Forget the struggle with those zips,
my rondeau round is now encased.
No muffin top.

# Abstract space at the dental hygienist's

*Recently, I tried to write a poem about abstract space, but struggled to understand what it might mean...*

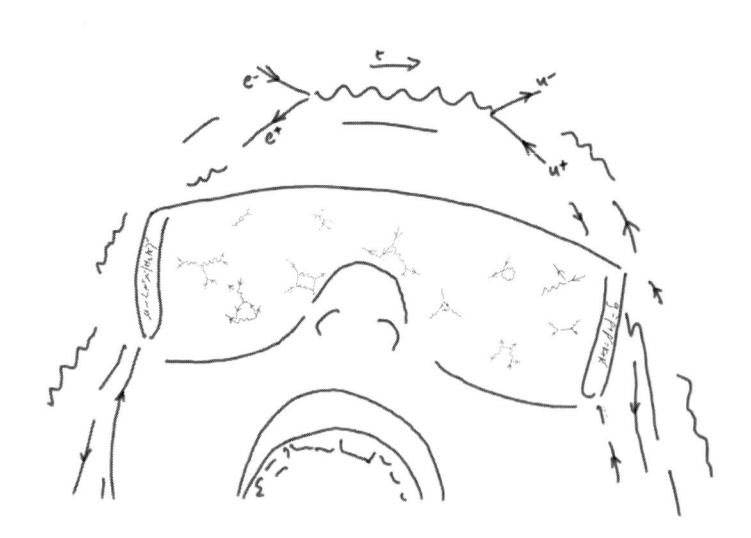

She's scraping tartar from my molars.
I'm wearing silly goggles, a baby's bib,
dribbling. Can anything be worse?
Yes, childbirth, but that's another story.
Think about something else.

Abstract space. What is it?
Can you have concrete space?
I don't know. My mind's gone solid,
cast in a concrete overcoat.
Perhaps it's age.
Ping. She's hit a nerve.
Think about something else.

In a foreign university room
my stepson writes equations on
a whiteboard. His space isn't abstract,
it's crowded with points of energy.
Quarks and bosons circulate,
gravitational waves ripple across
dark voids of space and time.
I should have been a better stepmother.

There's no space,
abstract or otherwise, in my brain.
It's full. Things get lost, fall out.
Is that down to age again?
Ping. 'Ow.'
'Open wider please…'
Think about something else.

# The Thoughts of Kumbuka the gorilla

*In 2016, Kumbuka, a 29 stone gorilla, escaped from his London Zoo enclosure and drank five litres of undiluted blackcurrant squash. He was tranquillised and returned unharmed. In the same week, Donald Trump was likened to a silverback gorilla by a supporter.*

Lounging on my log, I watch you simple
souls out there. How flattering to see you
push and shove, all to get a glimpse of me.
You assume you're better off, and free,
but if you read at all, I think you'll find that

Rousseau wrote that apes like me are
liberated, nature's truest men. Or, consider
Marx's chains, which could never bind
my free-ranging, uncorrupted mind. While
Hegel, on the other hand.... oh look,

one shouldn't tease inferiors, but how
can I resist? Carefully, I pick my time...
Then, while charging forward really fast,
I bare my teeth and punch the glass.
How those dreadful children scream!

Huh, flashes in my face. Deliberately I
scratch my balls then slowly turn away.
'Trump!' you shout, 'Let's see you, Trump!'
No trouble folks, I'll lift my rump...
Phew, sorry, that was rich....it's

all those gassy vegetables y'know.
Dieting is such a frightful bore,
it does nothing for my mood
and I'm just so obsessed with food…
A while ago I had tremendous fun,

some idiot left my gate undone!
What was an ape to do? Well,
out I'm strolling, cool as fuck,
couldn't quite believe my luck…
Poor keeper nearly shat a brick.

Now, I just love that ghastly purple squash,
although it's own-brand, rather cheap.
What am I like? It's artificial, sickly sweet…
but I swigged a bloody skinful, neat.
Whoa, sugar rush! I must have passed out cold,

next thing I know I'm back in here with extra
cake for tea. I scoffed it but my guts were aching,
to be frank. Then, I heard the loonies shout
'Return Kumbuka to the wild!' 'Let Kumbuka out!'
Look, I was born in Belfast. I've never known

another life. My home is here. You stupid humans
trashed our lands, turned our rivers into sand.
Out there I'd surely starve, or slowly die of thirst.
You'd steal my kids, or maybe shoot them just
for fun… Let Kumbuka out? No bloody chance…

# Thinking about smells…

sends my mind whirling
  like a flock of gulls
    after a dropped chip. Chips?
      Now there's a smell to savour.
        What about party poppers?
      Poppers? Not those little bottles
    passed around in dodgy clubs.
I sniffed one once, nauseating,
dry cleaners, petrol, burning rubber,
  instant migraine.
    No, party poppers. Pull the string, bang,
    streamers fly, inhale the smoke.
      Remember caps?
        Paper rolls with dots on?
        I'd fire my gun,
          breathe that smoky whiff.
            I was a little cowboy child,
            wouldn't wear a dress.
              Is it true that kids these days
              are free to choose their gender?
            Glad I wasn't asked.
      I'd have gone for 'boy'. Big mistake.
Men have to use piss-pongy loos. Him at home rolls up
his sleeve, reaches down the kitchen drain for clots of
smelly gunk, scrapes cat poo off the rug, swills stinky
stagnant water butts, kills maggots in the wheelie bin
  while I sit
    in the garden
      smelling roses…

# It's a frog's life

Come foolish girl, kiss me if you must.
Your lips can scrape my tender skin
with sandpaper caresses, but hear this,
I won't become a prince.
Transformation? I've done it once.
That was quite enough…

Once, my water world was limpid, cool.
All in black, I lived to eat and wriggle,
rooting in the mud for the corpses
of my siblings, so convenient to nibble.
Don't clutch me tightly in your hand,
the heat will make me shrivel…

You shudder. Why? Is kissing me so vile,
such an abhorrent test of love?
You know I need this coat of slime,
but please admire my jewel-bright eyes,
these translucent fingers, so like yours.
Watch my tongue. Zap! Goodbye flies!

Make up your mind, I've work to do.
A frog's life is stressful. Put me down.
Let me hop onwards, crossing roads,
gritty concrete, shadeless ground
to find my pond. Will it still be there?
It's drying up, getting smaller every year.

Kiss me if you must, but what a waste
of time. You'll get no change from me.
There's something I forgot to say,
I'm off to lay my eggs. Now can you see,
I could never be a prince.
Transition? Now that's a leap too far…

# Acanthus

We tipped her gently, folded into waiting earth.
A still day, no ashy cloud drifting on the breeze
to shock the neighbours. They watched us plant
a tender yellow rose, well-staked and watered in.
'Yellow means Remember Me,' we said.

I threw away the empty plastic urn,
tried to forget her final years, trapped
in a crumbling body until blessedly, her
mind departed, floating free. Finally,
nothing but an empty husk remained.

Next spring, the rose was shrivelled, brown.
I snapped off brittle bone-like twigs
and threw them on the bonfire.
At first, the earth lay bare, reproachful, then
shrugged on a shroud of soft green weeds.

Uninvited, a spiky star of leaves appeared.
An alien stranger pushed aside the soil,
erupted, expanded, a mass of glossy green.
Dark plant energy, with soaring from its heart,
a triffid wand, a twisted whorl of flower.

Acanthus. Old familiar from a darker time,
a pagan symbol of renewal, the eternal wheel
of life. Ash to earth, earth creating life again.
Crowding out the other plants, it dominates its bed.
'Forget that rose,' it shouts, 'Remember me instead.'

# Bed companions

I've shared a bed with cats, treadling, pulling threads,
hairy mufflers on the pillow, purring in my face.
Washing,
slup slup slup
scratching,
bip bip bip bip bip

I've shared a bed with dogs, wagging, circling,
tugging at the covers, dog breath in my face
Rootling,
roffle roffle roffle
scratching,
bam bam bam bam bam

I've shared a bed with kids, kicking, wriggling,
sharp elbows in my ribs.
'Mum?'
'Go to sleep'
'Gran?'
'Go to sleep'
'Someone's farted!'
Giggling,
hee hee hee hee hee

I've shared a bed with men, snoring, rustling,
beer fumes in my face, taking all the bedclothes.
Now I share with just the one.
Whispering,
sharing secrets in the dark,
loving,
dot dot dot dot dot

# Dot

Dot?
Yes. What's that?
A full stop is *point* in French. Press a
point to the page to make the smallest mark.
Dot. Full stop is German *punkt*. Press the point harder,
the puncture hole is space, not punctuation, although *punctus*
is full stop in ancient Latin. Full stops are periods in America.
It's Latin again, *periodus,* another sort of dot. What do Americans
call women's monthly business? Maybe they call periods full stops.
Dot dot dot... ellipsis weakly tails away, sniggering behind its hand,
diffusing words that might be rude. Periods are natural, not a hidden
bleeding shame. OK, no ellipsis. Period. Here, two dots: one above,
one below. Managerial colon holds a sentence back, then shoots out
emboldened pellets, line of bullet points. How explosively colonic.
Dot.coms always need their dots, and decimals need their points.
What a lot of meaning to a dot. Imagine a page, blank, with one
full stop in the middle. Could that be called a poem? Would it
be radical, rebellious, or just plain silly? What would be the
point of it. Every paragraph, every piece of writing,
all the books ever written end with a full stop.
This poem, this book both end with a dot.
That's what? Yes.
Dot.

●